I0645260

Braving the Shore

A Small Town Sisters Novel with a Sweet
Romance
Book One of the Soul Sisterhood Series

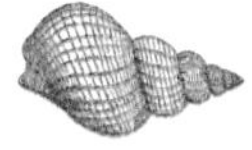

~

Cori Wamsley

Aurora Corialis Publishing

Pittsburgh, PA

BRAVING THE SHORE
Copyright © 2022 By Cori Wamsley

All rights reserved. No part of this book may be used, reproduced, stored in a retrieval system, or transmitted by any means—electronic, mechanical, photocopy, microfilm, recording, or otherwise—without written permission from the publisher, except in the case of brief quotations embodied in critical articles or reviews. No part of this book is to be used to train artificial intelligence. For more information, address cori@auroracorialispublishing.com This is a work of fiction. Names, characters, businesses, places, events, locales, and incidents are either the products of the author's imagination or used in a fictitious manner. Any resemblance to actual persons, living or dead, or actual events is purely coincidental. Any perceived slight of an individual or organization is purely unintentional.

Paperback ISBN: 978-0-9903174-5-6
Ebook ISBN: 978-0-9903174-6-3
Printed in the United States of America
Cover designed by Getcovers
Edited by Allison Hrip, Aurora Corialis Publishing

Praise for Braving the Shore

"Cori Wamsley writes an intriguing story, one she has artfully woven with the unbreakable bonds of sisterly love and the infinite connection to the spiritual realm."

J.D. Wylde
Author of *When Trouble Comes Calling* and *When Push Comes to Shove*
www.jdwylde.com

"Chelsea's journey of perseverance at all costs was inspiring. As a mom to two young girls, seeing the strength of her relationship with Jocelyn struck a personal chord. *Braving the Shore* demonstrates how overcoming great challenges and discovering your life's path is all the more meaningful when it's done alongside those you love."

Kimber Wood
@now__reading__kw book blog on Instagram

"*Braving the Shore* is a delightful story that shows us how important it is to listen, remember who we are, and make brave choices. It will be a great book for anyone needing a sweet, little nudge to be courageous, receive support, and claim who they are."

Gabrielle Smith Noye

"This tale of sisterhood, love, and how the Universe works in mysterious ways is one that won't soon be forgotten! The book was satisfying from start to finish—it brought all my senses to life; I could feel the ocean, smell and taste the goodies in the bakery, and see and hear the characters as if they were old, familiar friends. These real, relatable women could be any of us if the circumstances were just right. *Braving the Shore* is an incredible read."

Kelli A. Komondor
Bestselling Author of *Twenty Won*

"Cori Wamsley sparks intrigue in her newest novel *Braving the Shore* by bringing reality and the ethereal together to find balance in the chaos for the lives of identical twin sisters, Chelsea and Jocelyn. When the two sisters reunite, a traumatic event creates what feels like a rift in the amazing universe that they have known all their lives.
"Cori Wamsley is a brilliant and colorfully descriptive author whose writing of *Braving the Shore* draws in the audience, allowing the reader to feel like they are in the midst of the storyline. One may be able to experience the aroma coming from the bakery kitchen, feel the sandy shore as a peaceful refuge, see the colors of the sea glass and understand its symbolism of healing in the story, feel when someone's glance makes the heart flutter with glee, to name a few."

Sue E. Fattibene,
Author of *The Day the Angel Sat Beside Me*
www.suefattibene.com

Other Books by Cori Wamsley

Contemporary Fiction:

The Soul Sisterhood Series
    The Treasures We Seek
    Good in Theory
    Ashes and Other Inheritances

Business:
    The SPARK Method: How to Write a Book for
    Your Business Fast

Children's:
    Monkey Mermaid Magic
    The Knight and the Ninjas

Anthologies:
    Twenty Won: 21 Female Entrepreneurs Share their
    Stories of Resilience During a Global Pandemic
    Living Kindly: Bold Conversations about the
    Power of Kindness

"Manifesting is a lot like making a cake. The things needed are supplied by you, the mixing is done by your mind, and the baking is done in the oven of the Universe."
~ Stephen Richards

Chapter One

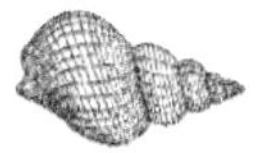

The wind was so joyous!

It had been a long time since Jocelyn just breathed and felt the openness around her. The last four weeks in Arizona were lovely, but honestly, she needed the sea.

She needed the caress of the wind on her face and in her hair.

She needed a boat and the feeling that she's about to embark on an adventure.

She needed the way the sea under the boat made her feel like she was bobbing freely in the air. Almost like being on a plane but with her own wings. The captain of her destiny. A soul on a mission—with the mission being to traipse around wherever she pleases.

Arizona offered her sand. Miles and miles of sand.

She'd never felt so dry. Or trapped.

Dry heat. Dry soul. Dry desires. Just dry.

It was an experience she's glad she had! But at the same time ...

God, you can't top water!

After all that time in the dry heat, with her hair piled on top of her head almost every day, Jocelyn really needed a change.

I'm glad I found that salon on the mainland. How lucky that one of my followers recommended her. Sierra was such a gem! A miracle worker!

Jocelyn had handed the fate of her head over to the stylist and closed her eyes. After chopping off over a foot of hair, Sierra managed to get that saturated deep red to go sandy blonde.

I'm glad for the transformation!

And for the first time in a while, I feel like I can slow down. I can breathe. It's like the sea is giving me life again.

Breathe in. Breathe out. With the rhythm of the waves. She felt the calm wash over her as she closed her eyes for a moment, letting the ship dip and bow under her as she gripped the railing.

Leaving the rush of life on the mainland behind her, and taking a well-earned vacation from her popular show, Jocelyn closed her eyes and felt the chill of the wind through her light-weight sweater, glad she had opted for jeans instead of shorts and ankle boots.

It's been too long since I've had my toes in the sand on Sorel Island for more than a couple days. Almost a decade. But it's time.

And it just feels right to do a big, long birthday back home with my sister. Thirty-five. Yikes.

I'm glad I have three weeks here! Who knows when I'll be back in the States again?

Jocelyn's thoughts turned to the next step in her journey. At the end of her vacation, she would be off to Germany to film the next show. Her assistant had already moved most of her belongings into a small apartment in Mannheim. Not that she had a lot of belongings. When you blow wherever the wind takes you, you don't take much with you. A few suitcases. A couple boxes of books and knickknacks that she loves.

Opening her eyes, Jocelyn noted that the island almost glowed, vibrant with life. Named for its chestnut trees, it exuded a New England warmth along with the ease of northern island life. Jocelyn sighed. Home. Sort of.

The sand stretched on ahead of the crashing waves, and she could make out some of the charming little houses and shops that lined the eastern shore of Sorel Island.

* * *

"I see the boat!" A little boy standing near Chelsea jumped up and down, jerking his mom's arm with him. He bumped into Chelsea in his excitement and looked up at her.

"I'm excited too." Chelsea grinned as she watched the vessel creeping toward the island. She could barely keep from jumping up and down herself. *It's been too long since I've seen her! A lot has happened. I hate keeping secrets from her, but I wanted to tell her in person. She has to see how happy I am!*

A gust of wind billowed her maxi dress, and she was glad she had thrown on her denim jacket. Chelsea wrapped her arms around her waist and breathed in the salty air. What an exciting reunion this would be!

The crowd at the dock jostled around as people tried to get in place for the return trip to the mainland, as well as a few like Chelsea who were waiting on loved ones. They were lucky that it was a beautiful and somewhat warm spring day in New England.

The boat was moving painfully slowly across the channel, but the onlookers could see the passengers on the deck now. "She should be easy to spot with that red hair," Chelsea muttered. She held her hand above her sunglasses to help with the glare from the late morning sun. "Is she on the boat?"

Pulling out her phone, Chelsea checked for any messages she might have missed and smiled at her darling daughter Karsyn's picture on the lock screen. Karsyn would be so excited to see Aunt Joss when she got off the bus that evening. Chelsea herself was bursting. "I guess she's on there. Maybe just not where I can see her," she muttered to herself. She rose up on her toes and squinted.

Then she gasped. *It's like looking in a mirror. Oh, she's going to be surprised!*

* * *

The boat docked, and Jocelyn gathered her bags, adjusted her straw Panama hat, and approached the gangplank.

She scoured the group gathered at the dock. A half smile crossed her face. Then she threw her head back and laughed.

"Twins indeed!" Jocelyn cackled. She threw up her hand. "Chelsea!"

On shore, Chelsea waved her arms in the air, jaw hanging open in surprise. "It really is you!"

Jocelyn practically ran off the boat, dropped her bags, and flung her arms around her sister. "I soooooo missed this!"

"Who ARE you?" Chelsea laughed. The two remained in their embrace but pulled back to get a good look at each other. "Where is all your red hair?"

"Gone!" Jocelyn laughed. "I wasn't expecting yours to be so much lighter. We almost match! That's quite a surprise!"

"I just did this a couple weeks ago," Chelsea played with her hair a moment. "I don't think we've done this since middle school." She grabbed one of Jocelyn's suitcases.

"And never by our own choice," Jocelyn responded. She grabbed her other bags and followed Chelsea.

"Mine has been shoulder length for a while now," Chelsea said, "so technically, you're copying me."

Jocelyn laughed. "I nearly shaved it all off the first day in Arizona."

"I'm glad you didn't," Chelsea said. "That looks wonderful on you! And it lets your natural wave come back in."

"Yep. Bounced right back."

Chelsea stopped behind a silver sedan and grinned.

After a moment, Jocelyn realized she was waiting for her to notice the car. "Oh ho! You got it! Nice!"

"It's been a long time coming," Chelsea said. "They finally put in a charging station in the Target parking lot, so I took it as a sign." She laughed.

"Well, I'm really proud of you! The Salty Cupcake must be doing really well!"

"Yep, I'm selling more treats every day than I ever imagined possible!"

Jocelyn walked around the car and touched the driver's side door.

"You want to drive it home?"

Jocelyn grinned. "I do! I haven't driven in a while, though."

"You'll be fine," Chelsea said. "But it takes a minute to get used to the braking. You just lift your foot off the gas slowly to decelerate."

"Is it still called a 'gas pedal' if it's electric?"

"You know what I mean," Chelsea laughed.

Jocelyn threw her suitcases into the trunk. "OK, I'm in."

The two climbed into the car and buckled.

Jocelyn glanced expectantly at Chelsea. "Keys?"

"No need." She placed her cell phone on the charging station. "It knows we are here because it senses my phone."

"That's a little creepy," Jocelyn says. "That reminds me though ..." She dug in her purse. "You probably won't need this now." She dropped something into Chelsea's hand.

"How cute!" It was a small rose quartz carved elephant attached to a key chain. She looked at the treasure and smiled.

"I picked it up when I was in Bali at their safari park. It reminded me of you."

"I love it!" Chelsea hung the key chain on her purse. "Now we won't get our purses mixed up."

Jocelyn put the car in gear and slowly moved forward, adjusting her foot on the pedal cautiously as she learned the car's sensitivity. "I didn't even think about us having the same purse or I would have used a different one."

"No worries! Take a left out of here."

Jocelyn guided the car onto the main road. They passed a few stores and restaurants but quickly ended up in the residential area. The houses were quintessential New England—Cape Cod-style homes or bungalows with siding in beautiful pastels, gabled roofs, dormers, and sweet little porches. An occasional Victorian was tucked into the neighborhood, withstanding the changing times, in brilliant dusty blues and grays, gingerbread frolicking about the porch roofs. That's something they both always loved about the island. It was beautiful and felt like a land tucked away waiting to be discovered.

Gazing around her with a warm grin, Jocelyn continued. "Did you know that the elephants at the safari park aren't native to Bali? Bali doesn't have any elephants. They were rescued from Sumatra."

"I didn't know that! Are they endangered there?"

"They are. It's pretty sad." Jocelyn accelerated. "Ooooh, I'm liking this car!"

"Yeah, it's a really smooth ride. No jerky acceleration."

"Anyway, there is a lot of illegal deforestation and poaching in Sumatra, so it's important that they rescued the elephants. Did you see my posts or the show about the safari park?"

"I saw part of it! Karsyn had it up on her tablet, and I was trying to watch while I was making dinner. She just loved seeing the elephants! And she can't wait to see you when she gets off the bus."

"Oh good! I cannot *wait* to see my little munchkin! Is she still doing pretty well?"

Chelsea sighed. "We've both been seeing a therapist since the divorce. Five is tough enough without your parents getting divorced as well." She could fill her in on the rest later.

"I'm glad you guys are at least friendly. I've seen some really, uh, dramatic divorces. The kids don't fare well when the parents are spewing hate at each other all the time. It's especially bad when it's behind the other person's back."

"That was Kate, right? One of your shooters? Can we please call them 'camera people'?"

Jocelyn laughed. "Yeah, it was rough."

Chelsea sighed again. "Yeah, I'm glad Damon and I are still talking. Honestly, it's just like it was when we were married. Just friends. But in separate houses."

"I'm glad you've still got me!" Jocelyn said. She made a right turn, accelerated again, and reached for Chelsea's hand.

"Always, sista!" Chelsea called out.

"Hell yeah!" Jocelyn answered.

Together, they enjoyed the feel of warmth dancing through the car. Jocelyn smiled.

"I miss this. I miss us. I miss the welcome that the island and the trees and the breeze and the New England sun always bring me. I feel grounded," Jocelyn said.

"You don't have to stay away so long next time. You're always welcome to come home."

Look out!

Was that voice in her head? A pickup turned into their lane and slammed them hard head on. The sisters' eyes met.

"Joss—"

Shattering. Honking. Hissing. Skidding. Screaming.

Their bodies jostled and strained against their seatbelts.

Jocelyn and Chelsea gripped each other's hands. *"Don't let go."* That voice in her head again.

The world spun. The car spun. Then stopped. Jocelyn blinked her eyes open and saw their purses on the floor by Chelsea's feet.

We bought our matching leather purses in Florence right after the divorce. Chelsea stayed with me in my third-floor apartment. We loved the tile backsplash. She hunted everywhere for the same tile for her new townhouse.

The air bags filled the emptiness around them.

Only the sound of a pounding heart filled her ears. "Chelsea," Jocelyn whispered.

Chelsea groaned and fluttered her eyelids. She saw blood trickle from a cut on Jocelyn's temple.

We ate ravioli at an outdoor café. And we talked to Zara a lot. Our link to her was so strong there. There were three for such a short time ... Jocelyn blinked long.

Chelsea groaned again.

Jocelyn's eyes blinked open. She saw her sister slump, cuts on her face and arms. She looked down at their hands. *"Don't let go."* Her eyelids grew heavy.

Chapter Two

Sirens. Bright lights. Loud voices.

Something wet on her arm.

Jostling. Bumping. Urgent talking.

Then nothing.

More bright lights. A whooshing feeling. Gentle touch. The feel of so many people nearby.

Soft voices in the distance.

Then nothing.

She didn't know how long it had been since her sister's hand was in hers, but it wasn't there anymore.

She opened her eyes, though she didn't want to.

"... so we're doing a CT scan," one voice said. "We won't know anything else until we get the results back."

She looked to the left in time to see someone pushing a bed with a person in it out of the room. Two people in scrubs whispered nearby with a man. A child clung to his hand.

She released her breath, not realizing till now that she had been holding it. Blinked hard. *Am I in a hospital?*

"She's coming around," a voice said. "Let's be gentle with her. You can say 'hi' though."

"Mommy!" the child rushed toward her.

"Karsyn. Dr. Spencer said to be gentle," a man said.

His voice sounded familiar. She didn't know how to feel about it.

"Mommy, I was so scared that you died!" Karsyn said. She grabbed the woman in the bed by the arm.

She gasped.

"Karsyn, she probably hurts," the man said. "Be careful." Then he looked at the woman in the bed. "I'm glad you're OK. Jocelyn got hit pretty hard, so they are running some tests."

"Jocelyn?" the woman said.

"Your sister," the man said. "Do you remember her?" He looked concerned.

"I ... I do," the woman said. She didn't look like she believed it though. She sat up a little more in the bed. "She was beside me ..."

"Yes," the man answered. "She was in the bed right here. They just wheeled her out for a CT scan. Do you know why you're here?"

"There was a crash." That she was sure of. "I was driving."

The man paused, like he was waiting for more, but when it didn't come, he said, "A pickup ran a stop sign and slammed into you guys. Jocelyn broke her arm and bruised a couple ribs. They also said she may have a traumatic brain injury, which is why they are doing the CT scan. It's why she's in a coma."

"Shit," the woman said. Then she glanced at Karsyn. "Sorry."

Karsyn burst into tears and buried her face in Chelsea's chest. "Mommy, I'm scared for Aunt Jocelyn."

"Aunt Jocelyn ..." the woman said. She frowned and petted Karsyn's head.

"Chelsea?" the man said. "Chelsea, do you remember us?"

"Sometimes there is memory loss with trauma," a doctor suddenly said. He approached the bed. "I'm Dr. Spencer, Ms. Beckett. I took care of you and your sister when you came in."

"And I'm Damon," the man said. "Your husband ... your ex-husband." He glanced away. "I brought Karsyn as soon as I heard about the accident. I'm listed first in your phone's contacts for emergencies. I was worried that ..." He trailed off.

"I'm fine," Chelsea said coldly. She stroked Karsyn's curls as the girl nuzzled closer to her. *Why didn't I see that truck?* She felt very strange, like she was floating in her body, not quite anchored in.

She laid back down, confused. Nothing felt right, partially because of the aches all over her body. They really must have been hit hard! Partially because something ... just didn't feel right. Like she wasn't ready to be Chelsea. Did her soul leave her body while she was unconscious?

Chelsea glanced at the table beside her and saw a purse there with a small pink elephant hanging from it. The elephant from Bali.

"There were elephants in Bali. Beautiful, majestic." She lay back down and closed her eyes, still stroking Karsyn's hair. The little girl held her tight. Damon sighed.

"It might be a while before she remembers everything with clarity," Dr. Spencer told Damon. "She needs to take it easy for a few days."

"I'm just thankful she remembers Karsyn. That's all that really matters," Damon said.

"That's the nicest thing he's ever said ..." Chelsea thought. Then she felt really mean for thinking it. It turned her stomach. He wasn't that bad. Or was he? Things just didn't work out. They fell out of love. If they were ever in love to begin with. It felt like she was looking back on their relationship through the eyes of an outsider. Like it was never even real. And it only ended a year ago.

"Still no response," a man in scrubs said. He was pushing a person in a bed into the room. Her head was bandaged so much that most of her hair was covered. Her lips were swollen. Her arms lie motionless at her side, the right one splinted and wrapped.

"No!" Chelsea cried out. She sat up again and reached for the woman in the other bed.

"Ms. Beckett, she will be fine," Dr. Spencer said. "These test results look good. She needs time to heal. And we will be monitoring her twenty-four/seven."

"Jocelyn ..." she whispered.

Chapter Three

A day later, Chelsea felt well enough to stand and walk for a few minutes at a time. She was sore and bruised, but nothing was broken. No lasting damage to her body. To her mind though ...

A short time later, Chelsea and Damon were seated in the front of his red Audi convertible, Karsyn in the back. All of Jocelyn's bags were in the trunk. They had miraculously survived the wreck pretty much unscathed. Chelsea's car ... not so much. It was totaled.

Chelsea sat stiffly with her hands under her thighs, trying to keep herself calm. Being in a car so soon after that wreck was wrecking her nerves. She rigidly sucked in air and breathed slowly out, telling herself that it would be a short drive and Damon is a good driver.

"I'm sorry if this wasn't what you had in mind," Damon said, distracting her from her panic. "I called your Aunt Dana, and she said she would check if Megan can help out this weekend. Dana and Warren are at the Grand Canyon right now, and your Uncle Eric and Colleen are whale watching in Alaska. I told them not to worry about it, since I'm here. I'd hate to interrupt their vacations."

"It would be great if my cousin can come help. I appreciate you being here though, till Megan arrives. Did you hear what happened to the other driver?" Chelsea said. She returned to her breathing routine. In and out. In and out.

"I saw it on the news," Damon said. He tightened his mouth and looked grim. "They life-flighted him to Sterling General. I guess he wasn't wearing a seatbelt and flew out the front window when he hit you guys. The video looked horrific. No idea how he was still alive. He didn't last long though. Pronounced dead a couple hours after he went into surgery."

"Geez," Chelsea said. "I wonder why he was going so fast ..."

"Me too ..." Damon said.

"I like the elephant on your purse, Mommy," Karsyn said.

Chelsea turned and smiled at the little one in the backseat. She immediately regretted it and grunted. That's achy.

"Oh, yeah ... I got that in Bali," Chelsea said.

"What's Bali?" Karsyn said. "Can I go?"

"You mean *Jocelyn* got it in Bali?" Damon corrected.

"Yeah ..." Chelsea said. Damon must be right since her memory was a little off. "Jocelyn went last year, I think. She gave me this."

"I remember watching her videos from there," Karsyn said. "I liked the elephants."

"Me too, hon," Chelsea said.

Chelsea's townhouse was on the other end of Sorel Island in a community of townhouses, just a block from the beach. It had been a dream of hers to live within walking distance of the ocean. And she had a view of the bay from her top floor. The townhomes there were all weathered grays and beiges that felt incredibly like they belonged on the New England shore: laid back, stately, warm, and homey.

As Damon pulled into the driveway, Chelsea felt like she was seeing it for the first time: the bench on the front patio with its brightly colored pillow, the wreath of hydrangeas on the front door, the gentle way the willow in the open lot beside her flirted with the breeze. Beautiful. She closed her eyes. *"Thanks, Universe, for getting me back here safely. Now let's work on Joss!"*

Damon hopped out of the car and started pulling bags out of the trunk. "You sure it's OK for me to stay here till Megan gets here? If she can."

"I need the help," Chelsea said. "I appreciate the offer."

"I love that Daddy will be here too," Karsyn grinned. She was missing a bottom tooth.

"Did you lose a tooth?" Chelsea said.

"I told you last week, Mommy." Karsyn put her hands on her hips and frowned.

"Karse, give her some grace," Damon said. "Remember that she's healing."

"Sorry," Karsyn frowned and hid behind Chelsea, clearly embarrassed.

Inside the townhouse, Chelsea slipped off her shoes and slowly walked up the first flight of stairs. For obvious reasons, she felt like she had been hit by a truck. When she got to the main floor, she felt like it had been ages since she had last been there. *That was a hell of a hospital stay!* She observed the open floor plan of the townhouse and appreciated how airy it felt in almond white. The living room was carpeted in pale beige with French doors leading to a patio, and the kitchen had lovely greige wooden floors. White cabinets and beautiful artisan tiles graced the kitchen walls, and the living room was simply decorated with a sectional, a few tables, and a media center ... and a pile of toys and books for Karsyn, scattered wherever.

The navy sofa called her name. She approached, collapsed, and pulled one of the seashell-patterned pillows to her chest. She sighed. This didn't seem real. A piece of her heart was at the hospital recovering with her sister. And the pile of toys was making her twitch. Did she really live like this ... so messy?

"Chelse, can I get you something?" Damon asked. He was standing in the kitchen pouring water into a glass. Karsyn jumped on the couch with Chelsea.

Realizing she was making a face, she quickly put on a smile. "Hot tea?" Chelsea said.

Damon opened a cupboard. "Wow, looks like you stocked up."

"Joss and I have always liked tea," Chelsea said. "I had to have her favorite here: lemon ginger."

"Want that one?"

"Yes."

Damon brought the hot mug to the living room. Chelsea dunked the bag in and out of the water thoughtfully. *Damon always did take care of me.*

Karsyn wandered off and came back with three Barbies.

"I called The Salty Cupcake and talked to Samantha as soon as I knew you were OK," Damon said. "And I checked with your insurance about a rental car. I thought that would help you out when you're ready. The insurance will need to talk to you about details though. They said you can have a car as early as Monday."

Chelsea frowned. "Thanks. What day is it?"

"Saturday."

She had picked up Jocelyn on Friday morning. "OK, for a moment, I was afraid I had been asleep a whole day."

"With the accident happening on Friday, I thought it would be hard to take care of the car over the weekend."

"Always so practical."

"I'm trying to help," Damon shrugged.

"I appreciate it."

"They were worried about you at work. Sam asked if she could stop by when I brought you home. It's up to you. You might want to text her."

"Sam?"

"Your best friend ... your manager." Damon looked grim. "You really don't remember her?"

"Maybe …" Chelsea frowned and sipped her tea. "I'll text her and at least let her know I'm home. Could you hand me my phone?"

Damon picked up Chelsea's purse from the table. The little elephant bounced gleefully against the side. "You remembered Megan, and it's been a few months since you've seen her. At least, you haven't mentioned anything."

Chelsea shrugged. She pulled out the phone, held it up for a moment, and gazed at the lock screen photo of Karsyn in her bathing suit, building a sandcastle. *Beautiful.* Suddenly, the phone recognized her face and opened. "Now how do I text people …"

"Are you having trouble seeing it?" Damon scooted closer. "Maybe we should have them check your vision at your appointment on Monday."

"No … I can't find the picture … button … thing."

"App?"

"App."

Damon reached across and tapped the button. Instantly, the texting screen popped up. "You have a lot of unanswered texts." He raised his eyebrows and appeared to be reading the names. "There's one from Aunt Dana."

"I'll get to most of them later. I just can't right now." Chelsea looked for "Samantha" in the list. "Hey Sam, just wanted to let you know I'm home. Not feeling visitors right now. Maybe tomorrow?" After speaking the text, she hit the arrow to send. An immediate response came through.

"Got it! Sending tons of love and light your way!"

She popped up Aunt Dana's concerned text and let her know she was at home resting.

Chelsea sipped her tea again as they sat in silence. Karsyn brushed her Barbie's hair roughly and chattered about getting dressed for a big event.

"So ... did you want a show on? Anything ... ?" Damon seemed unsure of what to do after checking off the list.

"I'm fine. Really," Chelsea said. "I'm thinking I'll just stay on the couch this afternoon. Relax. Watch Karsyn play."

"OK then. I will bring Joss's stuff upstairs and put it in the corner, if that's OK."

"Yeah, yeah. That works."

Chelsea stayed on the couch for the next couple hours, her thoughts flowing around hazily. She thought about the wreck, about Karsyn, about the awkward next couple of days she would have with Damon if Megan couldn't make it. The strange way she felt in her body. It suddenly occurred to her that she hadn't showered since the morning before.

"Damon, I hate to ask, but could you draw a bath for me and make sure I get in the bathroom, OK?"

He nodded. "Sure." Then he followed Chelsea up the stairs to her room where she hunted through drawers for some comfortable clothes.

"I feel like I have no idea where anything is. Nothing even looks familiar. Sorry this is taking so long." She finally pulled out a pair of ocean pattern Capri pj pants, a coordinating blue long-sleeve shirt, and some underwear.

"You're fine."

Chelsea sank into a tub of hot sudsy water a few minutes later, and it felt heavenly. Sunlight slanted through the high window in the bathroom, lighting up the whole room. It was a really elegant bathroom with a garden tub, and she felt like she was at a high-end hotel. *That's what we wanted to do when we planned this room. At least I remember talking with Jocelyn about it.* Damon had placed a huge fluffy white towel beside the tub for her, which looked simply luxurious. She sighed happily, finally feeling the grunge come off, but in the back of her cloudy mind, she was still worried. *When will this feel normal?*

After a bath and change of clothes, she nearly felt like she was back in her skin. "Damon, I'm coming back downstairs. Can you just make sure I make it OK?" He approached the landing and watched her come down.

Man, it sure is awkward relying on someone to take care of you after you're divorced. It's like asking a stranger for help. It felt like she didn't really know Damon. It gave Chelsea a prickly feeling in her stomach to talk to him.

"Are you good on the couch again? Need something?" He sounded kind but cautious.

"No, I'm good. Karsyn is hanging out with me. You can keep watching your show if you want. Or read. Or whatever." Just then her phone buzzed. "Megan, I'm so happy to hear from you! I'm good. I mean, I'm not good-good. Just good for someone who got hit by a truck."

"You got hit by a truck?" Karsyn looked panicked.

"It's OK. Mommy will be fine." Damon squatted by Karsyn and gave her a quick hug.

"Sorry," Chelsea mouthed. "Great, I'll see you tomorrow morning then. Thank you, Meg!"

"So, in the morning then?" Damon asked.

"Yeah, Megan said she can stay through Monday. She's off both days from the salon." Chelsea set the phone down. "Anyway, you can do whatever you need. I'm fine here."

"Actually, I wouldn't mind a quick walk on the beach to clear my head. It's been a stressful couple of days."

"Oh, I don't mind. Go ahead. Like I said, I'm good right now."

The phone buzzed on the end table, and Chelsea looked down. A name lit up the screen.

"Julian?" Damon read. His eyebrows were raised the same way as when he was looking at all her unanswered texts.

"No idea ..." Chelsea frowned. *Who is this guy?* The phone continued to buzz.

"I mean, sorry, it's none of my business. It's not like we're married."

"No. I really have no idea."

"I guess if you don't even remember Samantha, it makes sense." Damon paused. "You sure you don't need me here?"

"Go walk. You've been a big help. We can call you if something comes up." Chelsea looked down at her phone again. The voicemail message popped up. *I'll get it later.* She put the phone back on the end table.

"OK, please rest. Be careful. I have my phone on me." Damon walked back down the stairs to the front door.

As the door clicked shut, Chelsea frowned.

"Mommy, are you OK?" Karsyn smiled sweetly.

"I'm good, cupcake." But was she? She started going through the list of people she had forgotten—Samantha, Julian, all the people who worked at The Salty Cupcake. She couldn't remember her neighbors' names, now that she thought about it, though she remembered their faces. At least being in the end unit meant she only had one family to remember.

She started feeling jittery, like she wanted to run. Mild panic was setting in. It was scary not to remember. It was scary to feel like her roots were coming up from the ground again. Now that was a familiar feeling! She dug back into her brain, sifting through memories. What happens when she feels this way?

A film started playing in her mind. A clue from the past. She pressed pause and examined the features.

She was dressed in a style of clothing that was hip two decades ago. Felt like she was laughing, but it was forced. A boy was there, same age as her. He seemed ... sour. She pressed play.

He said something, tinged with sarcasm. She laughed again but felt the pain of it in her abdomen. Her heart felt empty. She wanted to flee. She could almost feel her roots loosening from the ground, shaking in the dirt. Preparing for flight.

Then the movie dissolved in a puff of smoke. Two souls no longer entwined. She had cut the cord, a while ago. But the memory was there, even if she didn't feel like the bad energy from the moment bothered her anymore.

Exhaling slowly, Chelsea came back to the present. *This is where I need to anchor myself.* She looked around. The walls were a tasteful shade of white. The couch navy blue. The TV hung on the wall above a deep gray entertainment center. Taking stock made her feel a little less like leaving.

And there was Karsyn, gazing at her with questioning eyes, but full of love.

Karsyn climbed into her lap and nuzzled her. "Mommy," she whispered, "are you sure you're OK?"

Chelsea smiled. "Just trying to find myself."

Chapter Four

The rest of the evening, Chelsea felt restless. She kept telling herself she was fine, just achy, but she continued to feel restless, verging on panic. *But I can't leave. All I can do is rest. It's like the Universe is forcing me to slow down and breathe.*

Instead of going outside, when she had the energy, she slowly paced around the living room, pausing to sit on the couch or the stairs on occasion. Karsyn kept her company the whole time, and they ended up finally playing several exciting rounds of Go Fish. Chelsea was thankful for the distraction, but every time they finished a game, her mind drifted. She was afloat in a new world ... her old world anew.

Again, her phone buzzed. This time, it was Aunt Dana, so she answered.

"Sweetie, I was so worried."

"I'm glad you called. I'm feeling a little better this evening."

"You had us really scared. Uncle Warren says hi."

"Hi, Warren. I don't want you guys to worry about me. Damon is here tonight, and Meg will be here in the morning."

"Thank God she still lives close enough to go help you. Trina and Tony are so far away we never get to see them. And that sister of yours. When she gets out of the hospital, I'm going to have a chat with her about her globetrotting."

"Dana, I'll be so happy when she gets out that I won't care about anything but hugging her."

"We will do that when we're back home, but she needs someone to talk sense into her. You and Meg are the only ones with any sense. Family is everything. And Sorel is such a beautiful place to be. I can't imagine living so far away that driving in is a nuisance."

Chelsea sighed. She was certain she had heard all of this before. Dana was loyal to the area to a fault. "Hey, I need to go rest. I'm glad you called."

Not long after, Damon brought back a pizza for dinner. "It's Saperi's. Down the street. We've been getting this for years."

"I don't remember. It's really good though!"

After two slices of mushroom and ham, Chelsea took her plate to the sink, rinsed it, and put it in the dishwasher. She leaned against the counter, admiring the pattern of the tile backsplash. Gold, orange, brown, and gray ... old world ... "Duomo," she whispered, satisfied.

"Sorry?" Damon carried his plate and Karsyn's to the kitchen.

"The tile pattern is called 'Duomo.' I remembered. Joss helped me pick it out." Chelsea smiled at the thought.

"It's nice," Damon said with sincerity.

"I remember why we picked it too," Chelsea continued. "We looked everywhere for tile that reminded us of the tiles on the cathedral floors in Italy. I just loved them when I visited Joss there." *After the divorce*, she thought, affirming her memory. She loved working with her sister on the townhouse, looking at pictures of furniture and paint and other things together via video conference. It was so much fun. *I wonder what she's dreaming of while she's asleep …*

"That sounds nice," Damon said. "I'll have to go there someday." He shifted uncomfortably. "Did you need help with anything? I was going to work a little in the dining room if you don't mind."

"No, that's fine." *Typical workaholic Damon.* "Do what you need to do. I'm going to rest and hang out with Karsyn."

"Daddy, are you building something?" Karsyn asked.

"I am!" Damon responded. *He loves talking about his work.* "It's a new home a couple hours from here. Single family, five bedroom. I'm still working on the top floor, and they need the proposal next week. Gotta keep pushing to meet those deadlines!"

On a weekend? Chelsea frowned at the wall so no one saw her. *You have to make time to enjoy your life. I guess this is one of the reasons why we didn't work out.* She sat down on the floor. "Karsyn, do you want to pick a game? I'd like to play something!"

"Yay! How about our favorite?" She opened a door in the TV cabinet and pulled out a huge white box.

"Our favorite? What is ... oh."

"It's Life! I want the red car."

Hmmm ... not my favorite. "I'll go with blue."

"Here Mommy. Here's your pink person. I want to be the rock star."

"Cool. Can I be the travel agent? I want to explore the world."

"No, Mommy. You're always the doctor."

"Oh yeah. I remember I wanted to be a doctor when I was little. Joss and I both did. We were going to do Doctors Without Borders and help people everywhere."

Karsyn cocked her head to the side. "So, you'd make sick people better? It sounds nice."

"It does, doesn't it?"

"Why aren't you a doctor now?"

Chelsea drew out an inhale and exhale as she thought about the question. Finally, she just shook her head. "I'm not sure. I don't feel like that would be a good job for me anymore. I know both of us changed our minds about it, so we didn't miss out on a dream. Don't worry!"

After getting her job, house, and husband, Karsyn started playing with all the extra people.

"Karsyn, it's your turn." Chelsea waited. "Karsyn, spin."

"I don't want to play anymore." Karsyn took two of the little cars and started loading them with people.

Chelsea snorted. "That's fine. Let's pack it up."

"OK." Karsyn dumped the cards and pieces back in the box. "Will you read to me now?"

Chelsea looked longingly up the stairs. "Cupcake, I want to read, but I'm really tired."

"Can I read to you? I have my easy reader books in my room!" Karsyn leapt to her feet and dashed for the stairs.

"Wait." Chelsea steadied herself with the couch as she stood. She still felt a little weak. "What if we brush our teeth and go snuggle in my bed? You can read me a story there."

Karsyn grinned. "Deal!" She raced up the stairs, followed slowly by Chelsea.

"Do you want some help?" Damon called.

Chelsea shook her head. "I'm good. Thanks though." She knew she had to get back to her life and would rather do it sooner than later. Karsyn needed her. Though she was thankful that Damon was helping, it just felt so awkward. And the whole house felt foreign. She almost felt like she was *his* guest.

The bed welcomed mommy and daughter with its flamingo pink comforter. Chelsea piled the decorative pillows on the floor, settled in, and pulled Karsyn close. She closed her eyes. They hurt. *Maybe tomorrow will be back to normal. But what does that even feel like? Darn this memory loss!*

"Mommy? Are you ready? You have to open your eyes for the pictures."

"Yeah. I'm good." Chelsea looked politely at the book, and Karsyn began to read.

Not long after, the pair fell asleep.

Sometime during the night, Damon came in. Chelsea felt the warm body next to her slip away like a specter and stretched an arm across the bed as Damon scooped their daughter up and took her to her own bed. Then he turned off the lamp and retired to the guest room.

A short time later, Chelsea dreamed it was morning. A woman stood in the corner of the room. *Zara?* The woman looked like her heart melted. She smiled softly and folded her hands over her heart. *I remember Zara!* "Do you have a message for me?"

Zara motioned to the mirror.

In the dream, Chelsea walked across the room and stood beside Zara. She looked in the mirror and saw only herself. *Zara never had a reflection.* She looked back at Zara.

Zara held up her palm, and Chelsea reached to meet her hand, palm to palm. A chill rippled through her body. Then, Zara looked around and frowned. She held up her other hand, showing her three fingers.

After a moment, Chelsea bit her lip. "Jocelyn is in a coma."

Zara nodded, and Chelsea assumed that meant she knew.

"Mommy?"

Chelsea gasped, and the dream dissolved into fragments. Zara vanished.

"Mommy?" Karsyn pulled on her arm.

Chelsea opened her eyes slightly and murmured flatly, "What?"

"Can I sleep with you? You were talking. Are you scared?"

Chelsea wrinkled up her face, confused. "Come here." She whispered. She threw back the covers and pulled the little girl to her. She felt love emanating from the two of them. It was the first moment since the wreck that she felt whole and happy. Together in one warm ball they fell deeply back into sleep.

* * *

Chelsea awoke to tingling in her right arm.

She flexed her fingers and heard a soft murmur nearby. Opening her eyes, Chelsea saw the little blonde head of her daughter resting on her arm. She wanted to lay still and watch her sleep, but that tingling …

Gently, she slid her arm out. Karsyn rolled over, curls tousled across the pillow. *She looks like an angel. How can a human look like that? Her breathing sounds perfect. How is this my life? How is she mine?*

The warm, stable, loving feeling of the night before slipped away and was replaced by a nervous jitter. A tear streamed down her face as a mix of emotions came flowing back. She was overjoyed that she remembered Karsyn, Dana, Meg, and Zara. But waking up in the middle of the night had been such a shock to her system. And then there was Jocelyn … and the missing pieces of her life. Chelsea rubbed her face, stretched her legs, and sat up. *I just don't feel comfortable.* It wasn't the same desire for flight that she had the night before, but it was a familiar feeling that was heading in that direction.

She tried to ground herself again. *Bed. Dresser. Lamp. Pictures of Karsyn. Karsyn herself.* She paused and reflected again on her daughter's beauty. Maybe that was where she would begin to piece things back together. Stabilizing herself with love.

* * *

A couple hours later, the doorbell rang. Damon jogged down the stairs to answer it, and Chelsea could hear him chatting with her cousin Megan about the weather.

Karsyn was down the stairs about five seconds later, just like a puppy. The doorbell means excitement. She kept interrupting the conversation, trying to tell Megan about her class pet and learning how to do a cartwheel and her favorite color.

Chelsea giggled and her heart swelled. She knew that Megan would help her out. Not that Damon wasn't doing a good job, and it really was kind of him to help, but she hated to rely on him when she wasn't doing well. Megan came up the stairs holding hands with Karsyn, and Damon followed her, insisting on carrying her overnight bag.

"Hey Meg." Chelsea approached her for a hug. She always looked so cute with her chic blonde bob and effortless style. Today, she had on a leopard print kimono over a red tank top with jeans. Her left forearm bore a tattoo of a dinosaur riding an asteroid, representing her two sons' loves: one was studying to be a paleontologist, and the other was in astronomy. Clearly mom is proud.

Megan gave her a huge embrace. "I'm so glad you're OK. When mom called me, I was pretty freaked out." She brought Chelsea over to the couch and sat down. "How's Joss?"

"Aunt Joss is in the hospital," Karsyn explained. "She got hit by a truck! And no one knows how long she's going to sleep."

"I see," Megan said.

"Same as yesterday. I called a bit ago," Chelsea said.

"And how do you actually feel?" Megan stole a glance at Damon and then at Karsyn, as if gauging whether Chelsea would be able to open up in front of them.

"Mommy is better today. She's been relaxing, and Daddy is here helping because she shouldn't be alone in case she falls down. Sometimes grownups fall down, and maybe they get hurt bad," Karsyn interjected.

"I heard about that, Karsyn! That's why I came to help too." Megan smiled.

"Where are Dylan and Nate? Are they coming to play too?" Karsyn asked.

"They are at college right now. Did you know that—"

Karsyn gasped and grabbed Megan's arm. "I know that dinosaur. It's a T. rex. I have one in my room. Come see it." She pulled on Megan, and Megan looked at Chelsea and shrugged.

"Go ahead." Chelsea waved them out of the room.

Damon turned to Chelsea. "You know, I can come back tomorrow when Megan has to leave. My work is really flexible. I can work in the dining room on Tuesday if you need help."

Chelsea let out a deep breath. She felt like she had been holding it all morning. "I appreciate your help, but I need to get back into things. And I know it's awkward for both of us."

"I'm just concerned," Damon said. "You were in a pretty major wreck. And Karsyn is only five. She's not old enough to take on anything you can't handle."

Chelsea got quiet to see how this felt in her body, but honestly, she felt like she wasn't going to need help after tomorrow. "Just let me see how today goes. I really do appreciate the help though."

"OK. I wrote the bus schedule down just in case you need it. And I also wrote down the address for The Salty Cupcake in case you don't remember. You can always use the GPS to get there."

"Thanks. That's really more than I expected." Chelsea paused. "I'm glad we're still a team in raising Karsyn."

Damon gave a sincere, closed mouth smile. "Me too. I'm going to pack up and get out of your hair, but promise me that you'll call if you need me. You're still my daughter's mother. You're important."

Tears welled up in Chelsea's eyes. "I appreciate that."

* * *

That evening, Chelsea was less sore and stiff—Megan had her do yoga, take a warm bath, and rest throughout the day, which did wonders. While Megan read a book to Karsyn in the living room, Chelsea walked back upstairs and out on the balcony from her room.

The sea. The smell and sight hit all at once, and suddenly, Chelsea felt like she could breathe again. Being that close to the ocean let her feel close to every living thing on the planet, like she could feel their energy flowing to her. It's invigorating. It made her feel alive.

Part of her longed to dive in. *Do I have a snorkel? Do I snorkel?* The snorkeling isn't good in this part of the sea, though. It's better in the Caribbean. *Wow, why do I know that? Maybe I should go.* Her mind drifted to Karsyn. *Someday ... someday soon.*

She started thinking about Jocelyn and Zara and the night before, but then her phone buzzed in her pocket. *Julian. Who is Julian?* She almost pressed the button to answer but hesitated. *Why am I so chicken? I can't even listen to the message he left last night.*

She set the phone on the table and watched it buzz till the voicemail picked up. The buzzing blended with the sound of waves crashing just a block away.

A beep announced another message. Chelsea glanced at the phone and then again at the sea.

Someday ...

Chapter Five

Monday morning. No real news from the hospital. "Joss is still stable and improving," Chelsea told Megan and Karsyn as she hung up from the call.

The two walked Karsyn to the bus together. Karsyn was delighted to hold Megan's hand again since she was their "special guess," as Karsyn called her.

"Megan and I will be right here at the bus stop when you get home," Chelsea said.

Karsyn bounced up the stairs into the bus and flopped in the first seat. She waved gleefully at them.

Back inside, Megan took Chelsea by both hands. "How about you start today with meditation? I didn't want to push you to do it yesterday, since you might fall asleep. But I know you are used to it, so maybe getting back into your routine will help you feel more like normal."

"Maybe you're right. I still don't feel like myself, though I'm a lot less achy."

Chelsea sat on the couch, determined to meditate … even though "determined" is a little forceful for relaxing her mind and letting in her deeper knowing. With only the tiniest shreds of memories, she couldn't piece her life together, and she hoped that mediation would help her reconnect with her truth ... whatever that may be.

Setting the timer on her phone for ten minutes—because, let's be real, she still has to get over to the bakery and figure out her life there too—Chelsea took a long slow breath. She closed her eyes and imagined connecting with Mother Earth ...

A couple minutes after she began the meditation, in her mind's eye, Chelsea was walking on a beach, and she saw something in the sand. It was bluish green. As she approached, she realized what it was: a large chunk of sea glass. She had seen it before, but where? Sitting in the sand, she stared at the sea glass and waited for an answer to come.

She realized that someone was there with her. Two people. Both women. Maybe Joss and Megan? It took a moment for her to realize that she was looking into her own eyes both times. *Joss and Zara.* She smiled at them. They smiled back. Together, the women said, "Take this, and know," before they disappeared.

Moments later, Chelsea was listening to her phone alarm tinkling. And she knew she finally had a clue. But how was taking a piece of sea glass supposed to help her "know"?

That would have to wait.

Megan appeared from the kitchen with two travel mugs of tea. "Anything good?"

"Not really. I feel relaxed though." What was the point of telling Megan about the sea glass? They all spent time at the shore as a family when they were kids, but Megan was ten years older. She wasn't really "hanging out" with the twins, and Chelsea doubted she would have anything special to tell her about the sea glass. She could always tell her later if it felt important.

"Maybe something will come to you later. I'm ready to drive you to The Salty Cupcake, but you have to promise me that you'll take it easy."

"I swear. I won't make cupcakes too hard."

Megan snorted. "Don't your employees make the cupcakes?"

"I don't know."

"Oh boy. Let's just get you there and see what's up. Hopefully the manager can help you out."

Thoughtfully, Chelsea descended the stairs, slipped on her shoes, and locked up. The rental car sat in the driveway thanks to Damon and Megan picking it up. She didn't know how she lucked into a bright blue Mini Cooper. It was pretty cute, and there was enough room for Karsyn in the back. She realized that she would have to talk with the insurance about replacing the Tesla, but that could wait another day.

First, she needed to remember how to get to work.

"I'm driving," Megan stated.

"Oh fine." Chelsea tipped her chin toward the sky, breathed deeply a couple times, and got in the passenger side of the car. *I can do this. Plus, being chauffeured around wouldn't be so bad.*

She pulled out the note that Damon had left her and punched the address into her phone: 136 Bayview Dr. It sounded somewhat familiar.

"You don't remember how to get to work?"

"Nooooo," Chelsea said.

Megan gave her a weird look. "Are you sure we should be doing this?"

"I feel fine. And the doc said I might have some memory issues because of the trauma of the accident."

"Yeah, but you go to work every day. You remembered your family. You remembered me, and we don't see each other very often."

"You've been in my life longer than The Salty Cupcake."

"Karsyn hasn't."

"I didn't say this stuff would make sense." Chelsea leaned back in her seat and fought tears.

"Chelse, if you want to go back inside and rest, do it. Listen to your body. I wouldn't expect you to pop in the bakery for at least a week after what happened." She pulled out a tissue out of her purse and handed it to Chelsea.

"I just want things to go back to normal," Chelsea sniffed and then set her jaw. "I'm going to work. Even if it's just for a few minutes."

"Oh you are stubborn." Megan laughed. "And we thought Joss was the stubborn one."

Chelsea playfully smacked her cousin's arm and set her phone in the dashboard holder.

As the map pulled up directions, Megan backed the car out of the driveway and headed toward the bakery.

Just fifteen minutes later, they pulled into the parking lot of The Salty Cupcake Mermaid Bakery Café. It felt like ages since Chelsea had been here. She looked up and down the block at the cluster of little shops and restaurants that faced the ocean, just across the street from the endless blue sea. The Salty Cupcake itself was in a gray shingled building and had huge front windows, perfect for customers to indulge in people watching as they enjoyed their drinks and treats.

A bell jingled as they walked through the front door.

"Good morning, sunshine!" a woman called from behind the counter. The café part of the shop was filled with people sitting alone working on laptops or in pairs having lively conversations over coffee, tea, and baked goods.

"Heyyyyyy … you?" Chelsea said. The woman had long brown hair pulled back in a braid over one shoulder, a big smile, and sparkling chestnut eyes. *There goes the idea that seeing this place would jar my memory. I think I've seen her before … maybe?*

The woman chuckled. She wiped her hands on a towel and walked around the counter to greet her. "You don't remember me do you? You look confused being here, like you came in the wrong place."

Chelsea's face brightened. "Actually, I thought the walls were yellow." *I DO remember it!*

"They were. We painted it six months ago. Karsyn wanted more pink, so we went with the gray walls, pink and blue accents." The woman gazed around proudly. "Honestly, I love it. Your kid has taste."

"OK, I don't remember any of that," Chelsea said. "But I DO remember the yellow walls, which is a great step forward!"

"Oh!" the woman said. "I'm Samantha. Is it OK if I hug you? I know you don't remember me, but God, I miss you sooooo much!"

"Uh, sure … just, I'm a little sore, so be gentle."

Samantha embraced her friend lightly. Chelsea smelled the warm smell of baking bread mingling with Samantha's light fruity-flowery perfume. *Not familiar at all. Not even smells are ringing a bell?*

"I'm sorry. I just don't remember much from before the accident yet."

"You're fine," Samantha said. "Ease back in. I took you off the schedule for the rest of the week, so any time that you're here, you can just process, relearn, see what you remember."

"Wow, thank you!"

Samantha chuckled. "Not a problem, boss." She turned to Megan and held out her hand. "I'm not sure if we've met before."

"Megan. I'm Chelsea's cousin. I just came in to help her for a couple days. I have to be back at work tomorrow, so I'm hoping she really is as fine as she says she is."

Samantha laughed. "I'll test her out today and see if she meets our standards. By the way, Chelse, when you come tomorrow, make sure you park on the side and come in through the kitchen door."

Chelsea looked surprised. *Should I know that?*

"You have a key. Let me see your key ring."

Chelsea pulled them out of her purse.

"There, the one with the cupcake on it."

"Makes sense." Chelsea laughed.

"I'll leave you guys to it, if that's OK," Megan said. "I'm going to check out the shops. I haven't been to Sorel Island in ages. Be back in a bit."

Chelsea followed Samantha through the door behind the counter and into a huge kitchen. Vaguely familiar. "I'm just going to walk around and see what I remember."

She walked the perimeter of the kitchen. She peeked in cupboards and in the freezer. Feeling a little out of place, she realized that she had no memory of ever baking anything here. She felt like an outsider.

"By the way, these cherries really need to be used. Did you want to bake something?" Samantha asked.

Instantly, an old memory flashed through Chelsea's brain.

"Did you want to bake something?" Grandma said. "I have cherries."

"Yes!" little Chelsea cried. She was probably eight years old. Immediately, a kitchen opened up in her mind. Chelsea ran to the pantry and started pulling out ingredients, her sister by her side.

Back in The Salty Cupcake, Chelsea replied to Samantha. "I do ... I just remembered something."

Opening the cupboard, Chelsea pulled out flour, cinnamon, cloves, sugar, salt, baking soda, baking powder, and walnuts. She turned to the fridge and removed butter and eggs.

Samantha set the cherries on the counter and grinned before she walked away.

Chelsea opened every door and drawer in the kitchen hunting for the right bowls, cups, and measuring spoons. Nothing was intuitive. She didn't remember where anything was.

At least I have this recipe. Her cheeks felt warm as the memory of baking with her grandmother fueled her. She could hardly wait to walk through the steps and see how much she really knew.

Like riding a bike, the recipe came right back ... Her heart pounding, Chelsea measured the dry ingredients into a bowl. *This feels right!* Then she plugged in the mixer and creamed the butter and sugar in another bowl. Cracking the eggs, she dumped them in as the mixer continued to swirl the batter. She let out a breath. *I remembered all the measurements!*

Finally in her groove, Chelsea poured the dry ingredients in bit by bit and blended till the batter was homogenous. She pulled the bowl and gently folded in the cherries and walnuts.

Like someone who had way too much coffee, Chelsea bounced across the kitchen and fired up one of the ovens. Three hundred fifty degrees. She remembered. She bounced back to the bowl and poured the batter into two prepared cake pans. When the oven dinged, Chelsea slid the pans in and continued her frenzy by making cream cheese icing.

Heart still racing, Chelsea mixed the icing and licked a beater when she was done. Damn. Perfect!

So why do I remember a recipe from twenty-some years ago but can't remember any of my current life?

When the oven buzzed, Chelsea removed the cake and set it on the cooling rack. The kitchen smelled heavenly. She closed her eyes and leaned against the counter. The smell was bringing in memories, but none of them concrete. Crisp fall leaves. Warm mugs of cider. Laughter with her sister. Then it was gone.

Chelsea grabbed her water bottle and chugged. She breathed in the scent of cake that hung in the air like a warm blanket, beckoning her to wrap up in it and just savor the moment. Her memories could wait. The smell was heavenly.

As she took another sip, Samantha came back in the kitchen. "Doing OK? Oh wow. You really are! Look at that cake."

Chelsea grinned. "Yeah. I remembered everything. It's my grandmother's recipe. Joss and I used to bake with her."

"I love it. And the cherry walnut spice cake is always a big hit here." Samantha paused. "You know what. Let's go back out front and look in the case. Maybe seeing some of the treats there will jar some recent memories."

Chelsea nodded and followed her through the door to the front of the store. She gazed into the case. Doughnuts, cinnamon rolls, cookies, croissants, macarons, cupcakes ... and she knew many of the recipes by heart.

Samantha turned to talk to a customer while Chelsea stared at the cinnamon rolls. Suddenly, the shop faded, and she was back in the kitchen at her parents' house. Her sister, mom, and grandmother were there, and they were all working on cinnamon rolls. Grandma held her hand and helped her sprinkle cinnamon and sugar over the dough. The girls helped Grandma roll the dough, and then Mom cut it into rolls. Mom and Grandma placed all the rolls in a tray, and Chelsea and Jocelyn covered it with a towel.

She remembered that the next step took forever. You had to wait for the dough to rise before you placed them in the oven. Wait ... for ... ever. Chelsea remembered leaning on the counter with her sister, lifting up the towel every few seconds to see if the rolls were big enough.

"Give it time," Grandma laughed. Chelsea heard that a lot when they baked together. Jocelyn laughed and ran off to play, but Chelsea huffed and looked under the towel again. "Patience, sweetie. It will rise. Give it time."

Chelsea recalled being frustrated with waiting for dough to form or a cake to cool so they could ice it ... really every step of the waiting process that came with baking. Jocelyn was always so much more patient.

Jocelyn could go play and wait to be called to put the rolls in the oven. Jocelyn could take weeks to paint a picture. Jocelyn could date someone for more than a month.

Chelsea was always flitting from one thing to the next. Leaving projects and relationships unfinished.

Sometimes, memories are brutal.

"Chelsea, it's so nice to see you back behind the counter," a woman was saying. "We were so worried. Our prayers go out to your sister. May she recover soon."

Chelsea shook herself out of her reverie. "Thank you. The doctors say she will be fine." *This woman doesn't look familiar at all.* She furrowed her brow.

"You don't recognize me sweetie?"

"I'm so sorry. I'm struggling a little …"

"That's OK." The woman took her hand. "Sometimes that happens with a traumatic event. It will all come back to you." She gazed meaningfully at Chelsea. "Give it time."

Tears welled up in Chelsea's eyes. She nodded and squeezed the woman's hand. "Thank you," she whispered. *Thanks, Grandma*, she whispered to the sky.

As the woman left with her box of doughnuts, Chelsea turned her back to the store and leaned on the glass case. The room started to wobble, and she sunk to the floor.

Clearly, patience, I know, but for real, this doesn't feel right. None of it feels right. Why do I feel so impatient, like running? I was settled and comfortable here. Maybe the car wreck jarred my feelings of flight? Maybe I've been in one place too long?

"Chelsea, do you need help? Are you OK?" Samantha was squatting by her side.

"No … I'm good. I just need to rest."

"I'll walk you to the side door. You can sit on the stoop there and get some air." Samantha helped Chelsea to her feet. "Cass, Iz, can you two keep an eye on the front? Jada, wipe down some tables please. I'll be right back."

Together, the women walked through the kitchen and out the side door to the stoop. It was in the sun, and there was a nice breeze. Perfect spring weather. They sat in silence for a few minutes as Chelsea stared off toward the beach. She could see a slice of it between buildings, and it was calling her. Maybe that was the next place to go. Maybe that's where she would regain her past. It felt right, and she was hungry for it.

You can't run very easily on the beach. Your feet sink in the sand, and you can only go so far from the shore before you have to swim.

But if you can't run, then you have to stay. You have to soak in the fears. The memories. The good and bad. You have to accept what has come to pass before and hope to grow from it.

And that means being brave.

Was she ready?

Samantha spoke first. "I feel like you're trying to rush your recovery, Chelse, if I can be honest with you. You were just in a pretty bad wreck. Heck Joss is still in the hospital. I know you want everything back to normal. But this is a big upheaval, and it's probably for a good reason."

Slowly, Chelsea turned to face her. "What do you mean?" Her heart was pounding. She knew this was important.

"Well, you're almost thirty-five. That's mid-life. And you've already had a divorce recently. Karsyn started kindergarten last fall. You moved. The business has doubled in the past few months. You mentioned maybe looking into a second location a few days before the wreck. Your whole life is being shaken up. It's time to pause, re-examine, make sure you know what you want. Then, when you're steady on your feet, that's the time to anchor in and go."

Chelsea thought for a moment. She never felt like she was steady on her feet. Her intuition told her that she wasn't a "wait for stability" kind of person. But was she? "This feels like new territory."

"It is! But isn't that what makes life exciting? New challenges. Change. Eh, but that's always been fun for me."

"Change I like. It's the unknown that I can't get into."

"If anything is predictable, it's that life is unpredictable."

Chelsea was starting to realize why she and Samantha were friends. She smiled.

Samantha hugged her. "You OK now?"

"I suppose so." She stood and gazed at the shore. One part curiosity. One part trepidation. Then she saw Megan approaching with her arms full of shopping bags. "I guess my time is up today. I have an appointment, so we should probably grab a sandwich and go."

"Let me know how it goes," Samantha said.

As Megan loaded the car, Chelsea and Samantha returned to the kitchen. A few minutes later, Chelsea joined Megan with sandwiches, which they ate at the picnic tables outside. Then they headed for Chelsea's doctor's office for her check in.

As they drove, Chelsea looked around her. The sea always stayed constant, but the buildings that lined the strand had changed since she was little. A strip of shops had been painted and repainted to fit with modern colors and trends. An old burger joint had burnt when she was in high school. Now, it was a metered parking lot.

Gazing the other way, though, she saw the sea in its never-ending dance, in and out, in and out.

When it was Chelsea's turn to be seen by the doctor, Megan stayed in the waiting room, reading an old issue of *Cosmopolitan* and giggling about a ridiculous article.

Dr. Fisher breezed into the room, her gray curls bouncing. "Chelsea, I was so surprised to see you today! I read the report from the hospital. Glad you're recovering nicely. Your vitals look good. Let's just check a few things."

Before Chelsea could say more than "hi," Dr. Fisher was palpating her lymph nodes, checking her breathing, listening to her heart, and checking her hands for tenderness. "Any bruising?"

"A few spots, but they seem OK. Mostly legs and arms. I'm not as achy as I was Saturday when I left the hospital."

"Good. Good." Dr. Fisher was looking at Chelsea's forearms. "Everything checks out physically. How about emotionally? How are you holding up?"

"Fine. I'm good. I'm glad to be home with Karsyn. Worried about Jocelyn of course."

"Was Jocelyn in the car with you?"

"Yes, she's my twin sister. I was driving, and she's in the hospital in a coma." Chelsea's face clouded, and she feared that the dam would burst.

Finally, Dr. Fisher slowed down. She sat on the edge of the exam table and took Chelsea's hand. "Oh sweetie. Let it out." Chelsea bit her lip and frowned, but Dr. Fisher wrapped her in a mama bear hug. The tears finally fell. "You're good. You're good. This is *not* your fault."

"I know, but I'm so ... scared." Chelsea admitted.

"It's OK to be scared, sweetie. I'm sure she's as much a part of you as you are of her." Dr. Fisher pulled back and patted her hand but didn't let go. "As much as I know you want to put on a brave face for your daughter and plunge back into the way you think things should be, give yourself some grace."

"Thank you."

Dr. Fisher smiled. "There was a note from the hospital about memory problems. How is that coming along?"

"It's OK," Chelsea sniffed. "I remember the important stuff."

"And what's important?"

"Karsyn, the rest of my family ... a few things from my past like baking with my grandmother."

"I'm sure they told you at the hospital that trauma can cause temporary memory loss. At this point, I'm not concerned. It's pretty normal, so wait it out. Rediscover who you are. Enjoy some rest with Karsyn. Don't push yourself too hard. There is nothing to be scared of."

"So I'm just having trouble adjusting to my life?"

"Temporary memory loss, meaning it will come back." Dr. Fisher typed some notes in her chart. "I'm praying for your sweet sister, dear. I hope she's better soon." She gave her another quick hug. "Come see me again in a month, sooner if you notice any pain, dizziness, or other symptoms."

When Chelsea and Megan returned to the car, Megan took her hand. "Your mascara is smeared. You OK?"

Chelsea popped the mirror down from the visor, licked her finger, and tapped at the stray black mark beside her eye. "I guess. I just got emotional in there." She filled her in on what Dr. Fisher had said.

"Are you blaming yourself? I didn't think that was like you."

"No, I feel like I should have seen the truck before it slammed into us, but it was a weird angle, I think, and Damon said the guy was going too fast. I don't really feel guilty." Chelsea flipped the visor back up. "It's more like I feel like I should be able to just snap back into my life. Like I'm a piece that fell out, and now I'm back in, but I don't fit."

"Girl, that's how I feel when I wake up after too much Jack." Megan started the car and pulled out of the lot, back onto the main road of the island. Chelsea cackled. "So everything is normal, right? So don't worry about it. You'll fit when you fit. And Jocelyn will heal up. And everything will be back the way it was soon enough, with just a little detour. Maybe this is your chance to change things up? Rediscover yourself and what you like."

"It's hard to go on a self-discovery mission with a kid at home."

"True. Well, if you need to check out and get in a new environment, my place is only two hours away. And it's kid-friendly. I promise. I wouldn't want the boys to come home for the weekend and see that I'm not a saint."

Chelsea laughed again. "I'm sure your tattoo didn't give it away."

"It's all about the boys. They don't see it as a mark of anything else."

They arrived back home just in time to get Karsyn at the bus.

Nothing to be scared of at all ... right?

That night, Megan fixed a simple dinner of chicken burgers and salads, and they spent the evening reading together ... when Karsyn wasn't showing off her cartwheels again.

"So, you're good if I head home? Ready to drive and everything?" Megan asked as she packed up her bag.

Chelsea shuddered as she thought about getting back in the car and quickly covered it with a cough. She didn't want to take advantage of Megan when she was fine with everything else. "I think so. If I need anything, I'll call you."

"Good. I can be back down here if you really need me. Or you can stay with me a few days, and Karsyn could stay with her dad so we don't disrupt school."

Megan zipped the bag. "I really would stay longer, but I have a full day tomorrow, starting with a cut and color at nine a.m."

That night, after Chelsea tucked Karsyn into bed, she checked her phone. Another message from Julian. She went out on the balcony of her room and finally mustered the courage to listen. She played the one from Saturday. Then Sunday. Then today.

A new wave of panic set in. Each message sounded more worried than the last.

It's been three days, and he's called every night. *Who is this guy? Why is he so concerned?*

And why does he end every message with "I love you"?

Chapter Six

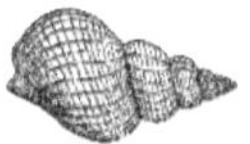

Tuesday. Another morning after a confused night of sleep. Chelsea woke up to her alarm in the middle of a dream where she had been on the boat to the island. Right before she was jolted awake, she had been floating aimlessly, stuck almost close enough to jump off and wade to shore, but continuing to drift. *Isn't that my life? Maybe I'm here. Maybe I'm there.* She was so close to remembering more sometimes, but there was an invisible barricade. Maybe her brain was trying to tell her something.

As she brushed her teeth, she remembered that someone else had been on the boat. Zara. This was the only part that made sense. Zara was always there when she was struggling. At least that felt normal.

She changed into her clothes and walked across the hall to wake Karsyn.

Chelsea sat on the edge of the bed and smiled. If nothing else, when she saw her daughter's face, she felt a surge of love, calm, and peace that told her that everything would be OK again. She thought of her sister lying in the hospital bed.

Hopefully sooner than later. We miss normal.

"Morning, Mommy."

"Morning, baby."

A short time later, Chelsea was again watching Karsyn walk up the steps of the bus. She stared after her, the only part of her story that felt normal, whole, safe. *How is it that I let a piece of my heart do this every day?* It felt strange to say goodbye every morning. She knew it was the way things go, but she wondered if this was a new feeling or if she had this surge every day that year.

Before the wreck.

Her life was divided into before and after. Some of the pieces of long before were drifting back in, like sea turtles returning to shore to continue their life cycle. But most memories remained lost, adrift.

She shuddered. *How long until this all feels normal?*

Chelsea waved as the bus left and then climbed into the Mini. She smiled as she looked down and noticed her pants. She particularly liked her outfit today. It felt breezy and beachy. Chill. Lilly Pulitzer capris and a white top with a ruffle. She felt closer to Jocelyn in this. It seemed like her style.

She pulled into the side lot of The Salty Cupcake beside another car and let herself in the correct door. In the kitchen, she found Jada and Isabel prepping treats. Two women she didn't recognize were behind the counter taking orders.

"Good morning," Chelsea called to the ladies in the kitchen. She looked around, uncertain of what she actually needed to do. Peeking in the walk-in fridge didn't jar anything for her. When she closed the door, she leaned against it and pursed her lips. *What now?*

Jada locked eyes with her and looked like she was about to say something. Chelsea grinned and glanced around the kitchen.

"Not sure what to do?" Jada asked.

Chelsea nodded.

"The chart usually lists what we need to make." Jada pointed at the wall. "Samantha said we are super low on brownies if you want to start with those. I already prepped dry ingredients. The recipe card is on the counter." She nodded toward the location.

"Thank you! I'll start on that. Hopefully the memory issue is temporary."

"It's OK. Don't be hard on yourself."

Chelsea sighed. *It's easy to say that, but how do I make that happen? I just want my life back.*

Without looking at the recipe card, Chelsea pulled eggs, butter, and milk from the fridge. She creamed the butter and sugar and added the eggs, milk, and vanilla. On autopilot, she continued through the recipe, turned on the oven, and poured the batter into a prepared pan. When the oven dinged, she slid the pan in and set the timer.

Another Grandma recipe. That makes it simple. But why do I remember these recipes so well and nothing from my recent life?

Samantha entered the kitchen then and seemed to read her mind. "Good morning, Chelse! Keep baking, and I'm sure things will come back to you."

Geez, my feelings are written all over my face. "I hope so!" Chelsea sighed again. She pushed through the doors to the dining area and stood behind the counter for a moment. As customers came in, she greeted them, acted like they were familiar if they seemed to know her, and busied herself with going over the different items in the display case. It looked simple enough, and she was pretty sure she had made all of them with her family before.

A piece of cake! Ha!

"Hey, by the way, you may recall that we keep a list of the product rotation by month, so we always know what to make in the morning." Suddenly, Samantha was by her elbow with two coffees, which she set on the counter. "Merilee! Natalie!" she called.

"I actually don't recall but thank you." Chelsea smiled appreciatively.

"You're welcome." Samantha squeezed her shoulder. "No worries. Hey, Greg! It's great to see you! The usual?" She was talking to a man who had just walked up, so Chelsea picked up the binder that Samantha had pointed to.

"Chelsea?" another man said. He had a warm baritone and sounded relieved.

Chelsea looked up. "Hi?" She locked eyes with him and melted. *I hope this is Julian ...*

"I'm glad to see you're here," he said. His big smile lit the whole room. "I heard you were in an accident."

"Uh, yeah," Chelsea shook herself from the spell. "I'm doing a lot better. Still a little stiff. But glad to be back, for sure." *That hair ...*

"I bet," he continued. "How's your sister?"

"She's still in the hospital. Improving every day, though. Thanks for asking."

"That's good." He looked like he was about to say something else and then changed his mind. "Anyway, it's my turn, so ..."

"Yeah, did you want something from the case?"

"A cinnamon biscotti please." He looked at the cashier. "And a medium coffee with cream and sugar."

Chelsea bagged the biscotti while the cashier handled the transaction. Her heart pounding down the wall of her chest, she struggled to think of a way to figure out if he was indeed Julian.

"Nice seeing you Chelsea! I hope your sister gets better soon!"

"Thanks! Have a good one!" *And moment missed. Shoot! He didn't say, "I love you," but that might not mean anything. Maybe he doesn't say it in public. Or maybe he was in a hurry. Or maybe—*

As the door jingled behind him, Chelsea turned and practically ran to the kitchen. Not missing anything, Samantha bounded in behind her.

"Hey, so what was that?" Samantha said.

"What was—?"

Samantha gave Chelsea a look. "Seriously. You didn't think I would notice that the room temperature went up like ten degrees when you were staring at him. Should I check your pulse?"

"Who was that? Do I know him?" Chelsea put her hands on her face. She knew she was red. *What just happened?*

With a savage grin, Samantha crossed her arms. "Oh, this is too fun." She cackled.

"Please help me." Chelsea looked at her pathetically.

"Fine. You really don't know who that was?"

"Julian?" Chelsea cocked her head to the side, seriously clueless. She crossed her fingers though.

"You don't remember Julian?"

Chelsea closed her eyes and shook her head.

"Oh boy." Samantha bit her lip and gazed at the ceiling before turning back to Chelsea. "That was Adrian, one of our regulars. Julian is your boyfriend."

"Oh shit."

"Yeah. So you haven't talked to Julian since the accident? That explains why he rushed in here frantically looking for you yesterday. I said I'd let you know he had stopped by ... and I totally forgot to mention it, sorry."

"No ... I haven't talked to him." Chelsea's head was spinning. *So it at least makes sense for him to end calls with "I love you." How long have we been together?* "I don't know anything about him at all. I didn't see any pictures out at the house. Karsyn didn't mention him and neither did Damon—"

"Of course they didn't mention him. They don't know about him!" Samantha said.

"Wow! Why?"

"You've been together officially since January. You met right after the divorce went through last fall. You haven't introduced him to Karsyn yet because you're protecting her ... you know, just waiting till the right time for them to meet in case things don't work out."

"That makes sense."

"Oh my God, I can't believe you don't remember him. And you clearly don't know what he looks like since you thought Adrian was Julian."

"I take it they look very different."

Samantha let out a chuckle. "Yeah. They do."

Chelsea frowned.

"It's not bad. Julian is good looking too. Don't worry." Samantha chuckled. "You know what else is funny? Adrian comes in here all the time and talks to you, and you've never *reacted* to him before. Never even gave him a second glance. Just polite, friendly shop owner stuff. Maybe that wreck jolted something loose."

"Probably a few screws ..." Chelsea muttered. *How can I have a boyfriend I don't even know about? And how did I never react to Adrian before? He's ... wow.*

"He always looked at you a certain way, but I don't think you ever noticed. I thought it was because you were pretty wrapped up in Julian." Samantha leaned against the door to return to the front. "The wreck definitely shook you up."

When Samantha left, Chelsea put her hand on her pocket where her cell phone was. Now she felt really guilty.

I can't remember my own boyfriend ... but all those recipes just came flooding back. Why not him?

"Maybe I have a brain injury too," she whispered. She wrote "Went for a walk–C" on the marker board and exited through the side door. She crossed the street to the strand, pulled off her sandals, and sunk her feet into the sand. *This is the only thing that makes total sense.*

Chelsea strolled along, letting the ocean lick her ankles.

The recipes were from before. A long time ago. She recalled her grandmother teaching her to make biscotti. "This recipe has been passed down for generations," she told the girls. "From the Donatos to the Marinos to the Caros to the Agostis to the DeLucas to the Biancos to the Blooms. It's yours now."

As she walked along the shore, a wisp of memory dredged itself up from the past.

"Grandma, I don't understand why it still hurts. I know I don't want to be with someone like that." She dipped a chocolate biscotti in a fresh cup of coffee. Even by the sea, she could still smell the mix of chocolate, java, and her grandmother's light flowery perfume.

"Just because it isn't a good fit doesn't mean it isn't going to hurt, love. You'll be able to let him go. Just keep telling yourself it was the right decision. You don't need someone controlling you like that. You're brave and brilliant and kind. You have a good heart. You'll make a lot of yourself as you grow. I'm already proud of the woman you've become."

Chelsea stopped and clasped her hands together as if she could hold onto that moment of memory. The last fleeting second of it was a feeling that she already knew had woven itself throughout her life, even if she couldn't remember most of it—the desire for flight. A feeling beyond wanderlust. A desire for escape. To run away and be someone else, somewhere else. Like wearing an ill-fitting suit jacket.

As the last breath drifted away, she sent love with it to her grandmother. *Grandma would have all the answers. She always did. She always will.*

She turned and began walking back down the beach, closer to The Salty Cupcake. As she did, she nudged the memory. She knew it had to be about the boy from the last old memory she pulled out. She sensed that he was controlling, demanding, especially after what Grandma said.

"You don't need to tell your sister everything. She doesn't believe you anyway." A man's voice echoed in her head.

That was him. And that made her want to run.

Fast-forwarding, she tried to piece together some more of her history, but it wasn't coming. What about happy memories? There were some vacations, maybe. Of course, those would be the most memorable pieces. She remembered moments of her wedding to Damon. Holding Karsyn after she was born. Fleeting moments like birthdays. Opening the bakery ...

But this *year* should be more familiar, memorable. She had a whole new life to celebrate after the divorce. A new home. A new boyfriend. *Where was it? Where was Julian in all of this?*

It's like most of her life was in pictures, except for the past few months. She didn't even recall picking out anything for the townhouse except when she and Jocelyn were looking at tile.

Chelsea groaned out loud and scared a flock of seagulls into flight. *Samantha was right. I need to breathe and give this time.* Again, her hand moved to her pocket. *I'll have to talk to Julian. Soon.*

She pulled out her phone and sat on a bench. 11:11, time to make a wish. Maybe he was taking a lunch break. She gazed out at the ocean. The crashing waves didn't hold an answer, not that she expected them to. She watched them a moment more. Maybe it was time.

Chelsea's heart thundered in her chest. Her palms got sweaty. *OK, I can do this.* Pressing on his name, she barely got the phone to her ear before he answered.

"Chelsea! I've been so worried about you! I saw an accident on the news, and it looked like your car, and then when you didn't answer texts or call me back … God, I'm so glad you called."

"Julian?" She wasn't sure what to say. His voice sounded nice, but definitely not familiar. *But how?*

"Is everything OK?"

"That was my car." Chelsea began, still wondering how to roll all the emotions and confusion into a simple phone conversation.

Julian exhaled loudly. "I was worried it might be. I know you didn't want me to come to the house if Karsyn was there."

"Yeah, I know. And thank you." Chelsea at least felt comfortable talking to him. Maybe this was going to be OK.

"I finally just stopped by the bakery, but you weren't there, and Samantha said ... Are you OK? Was Karsyn with you?"

"I'm fine, just shaken. Karsyn was with Damon. But Jocelyn was in the car too because she just got to Sorel Island. She's still at the hospital because she's in a coma." Chelsea let a slow breath out and stared at the waves. In and out. In and out.

"How ... I'm glad you're OK. Can I see you? I just want to hold you. You really scared me."

Chelsea bit her lip. She listened to the waves rolling.

"Are you still there?"

"I'm sorry. This is going to sound weird, but I just don't remember you." *Wow, I sound like an ass.* Hurriedly she added, "I'm having memory problems. I don't remember anyone at the bakery either. Not even Samantha."

"Oh." Silence.

"I know this is strange."

Silence. "It is. But maybe we can work on this together?"

"I'd like that. Clearly, you were important to me before. Maybe you can help me remember."

"I love you, Chelse. Of course, I'll help you remember. What would work with your schedule with Karsyn?"

Chelsea's mind was completely blank. *Schedule with Karsyn?* Of course, there was a schedule. She was co-parenting! *But what was it?*

"This might be weird too," she said, "but I really don't know. Let me check with Damon to see how we were handling things. He was helpful this weekend with Karsyn. I'm sure he will have an answer. I'm sorry, but that's the best I can do right now."

"I understand," Julian said. "Hey, I need to go now. I have a client coming in after lunch, and I need to wrap up some things and actually eat."

"That's OK. I'll let you know what I find out."

"Call me later. I love you."

"OK, bye." *OK, bye? Should I say, "I love you"? Probably not. What the hell is my life?*

Chelsea walked back to the bakery, erased the note on the board, and caught Samantha's eye as she exited the walk-in with a cake. "I'm going to the hospital to see Joss."

Samantha nodded and kissed the air. "Give her my love!"

First though, Chelsea returned to the townhouse. In the living room, she grabbed photo albums from the past two years and put them in her tote. Then, she jogged back down the stairs and headed for the hospital.

In Jocelyn's hospital room, Chelsea sat down beside her sister and sighed. *Five days. Five. Long. Days.* "When are you coming back to us?" She clutched her hand with both of her own. It was warm, but Jocelyn didn't respond at all.

"I brought some albums today. I thought we could look at them together," Chelsea said. She opened to the first page of last year's album. It was last January. A few pictures of Chelsea and Damon were scattered throughout the album, but never together. "Here's me celebrating our thirty-fourth last May!" Chelsea looked closer at the picture. She looked tired, worn down. Beside her, Samantha looked the picture of health and happiness, even though she had a six-month old at home at the time ... along with two other boys a little older than him—details that Samantha had shared to help with Chelsea's memory. But there she was, full of joy.

Chelsea knew this was a few weeks after she and Damon had agreed to separate. She closed her eyes and tried to get inside her head in the picture. Like leaves fluttering from a tree, she caught glimpses of her life at the time, all like she was watching the scenes unfold outside of her body. Around that time, she questioned whether this was the best decision. If she should just accept that Damon liked to work a lot and wasn't that into, well, anything else. If they should just stay together so Karsyn had both parents at home.

Karsyn had been destroyed when she found out. Chelsea was lucky that Damon had been pretty complacent with whatever she asked him to do. He usually was anyway. And the two of them agreeing to stay in the same area and co-parent Karsyn was best for all of them. They even helped each other pick townhomes that were a few minutes' drive from each other so Karsyn could maintain her school district, friends, and bus route regardless of who she stayed with that week.

The divorce and setting up for life afterward were almost easy, now that she looked back on it. "I guess we all learn to cope."

A couple pages later, and she was looking at Karsyn's birthday party. They used the clubhouse in Chelsea's community for it. Pizza, cake, games. It looked fun. Not bringing up any memories, though. She couldn't even recall any of the kids in the picture besides Karsyn. Wait. "Those are Samantha's older boys: Archer and Malcolm," she told Jocelyn. She recognized them from a picture on the bulletin board above Samantha's desk at work. Chelsea pointed, though she knew Joss wasn't looking.

Later in the book were a handful of pictures from her quick trip to Tuscany with Joss. "Oh, these are so great! It's been a while since I've looked at these. Joss, we had such a great time! I want to go back. I just want to forget about this accident and go exploring with you again!"

She touched the picture of the pair doing a selfie with a gorgeous vineyard sunset behind them. The whole moment was golden. She gazed at her sister. "I hope it's not gone forever," she whispered. "I wanted to stay like this a long time, just us sisters without a care, exploring the world, but I had to get home." *That feeling of flight ... Anyway, Jocelyn got to go back this spring for a short stint for her show. The images were breathtaking.*

"Maybe we can go somewhere else later this year. Wherever you're filming. Let's make it a date!"

Continuing to flip through the album, Chelsea smiled at all the pictures of Karsyn from later that fall, from Christmas. Getting her first roller skates and a much-loved new doll.

Frowning, Chelsea flipped back to the beginning. The album was almost entirely Karsyn, of course. A few shots of her with each of her parents, her grandparents, and cousins from Damon's side ... Very few shots of Chelsea doing things by herself ...

And none of her with a man other than her cousin Tony who had visited while he was in town for a family vacation.

"So, I don't even have any pictures with Julian. Joss, this is all so confusing!" She filled Jocelyn in on Julian. "I have no idea how this is going to play out. I wish you were awake so I could talk to you. That always helps."

Chelsea groaned and clenched her fists. Then she looked at the time on her phone. "Gotta go. Love you." She kissed her sister and left the hospital, arriving at home a short time before the bus and greeting Karsyn when she arrived.

"Mommy! Today was a great day!" Karsyn held out a paper in her hand. "I got caught doing good! I got an award!"

All thoughts of her own troubles were shoved aside. Happy face for Karsyn. "Karsyn, I'm so proud of you!" Chelsea grabbed her daughter and squeezed her tight. She led her inside. "You know what? Let's celebrate! How about a picnic dinner on the beach?"

Karsyn dropped her book bag on the floor. She looked shocked. "But we don't do the beach at dinner time on school nights because I want to play in the sand too long and get a bath late."

Thoughts raced through Chelsea's head. *Of course, the child would remember every little thing ...* Then she relaxed. A warm smile spread across Chelsea's face as she looked into Karsyn's sweet, innocent little blue eyes. "Thank you for being such a good helper and reminding me of that. But ... I think we need to make exceptions sometimes. Life is too precious and short not to enjoy a beach picnic every once in a while on a school night, especially when we have something *this important* to celebrate!"

Karsyn gave her a funny look and then raced upstairs for her bathing suit.

They gathered their picnic and beach things and loaded the beach wagon. Chelsea grabbed Karsyn's hand and wheeled the wagon down the block to the beach. Inhaling deeply, she gave the sea her worries and enjoyed the feel of complete and utter delight that the sand gave her. The shore was definitely feeling more like a refuge.

"Let's build a sandcastle!" Karsyn said.

The two trekked close to the water and began their creation with the wagon parked nearby. Gathering a bucket of water, Chelsea watched Karsyn scoop a pile of moist sand to form the base. Then, the pair dunked shovelfuls of sand into the bucket and fished them back out with their fingers, letting the soppy sand drip like stalagmites on the mound. Soon, an eerie collection of towers rose toward the sky as they worked quietly.

A short time later, they enjoyed their sandwiches, chips, cucumbers, and lemonade. While Karsyn played after dinner, Chelsea stood and wandered nearby, peering at the surf, the shells that had washed up, and anything else that reminded her this was a completely different world from her worries.

She bent down and ran her hand over a pile of shells that were surprisingly in good shape after being battered by the waves. That's when she saw the chunk of green sea glass. The sun glinted off of it as she bumped it with her hand. Lifting it up, she saw that its rough edges had been worn mostly smooth.

Warmth spread over her body like golden honey. And then a memory. "We used to collect this."

As children, Chelsea and Jocelyn thought sea glass was magical. Aunt Dana once said it was from a mermaid's tea set, and their mom encouraged the fantasy. Whenever they were together, Mom and Dana would spin tales about the mermaids drinking tea on the rocks in the bay and losing the cups in the sea. The girls had a whole giant pickle jar full of sea glass by the time Chelsea went to college and Joss went to ... find herself.

"But why didn't she come with me?"

She knew the pickle jar was at the townhouse now since Joss traveled the world. It sat in the TV cabinet on a shelf with the photo albums.

But there's something else ... where else was sea glass?

It was a big chunk. Huge. In the meditation with Megan.

A thought washed over her. Maybe it was an answer. *Sea glass is a symbol of renewal and healing.*

"Maybe I'm getting there. Maybe Joss is too." Chelsea looked at the sea glass in her hand. "Maybe she needs this."

Watching Karsyn playing, Chelsea suddenly felt peace. "Maybe I needed this," she whispered.

"Mommy, what's that?" Karsyn came over to look at it.

"Sea glass." Chelsea paused. "Did I ever tell you that this is from a mermaid's tea set?"

Karsyn gasped. "Really? Did you meet a mermaid?"

"I've heard the stories about the mermaids of the bay drinking tea on the rocks out there. I named the bakery after them. Would you like to hear about them?"

"Yes."

"Once there were three mermaids, all with silvery hair, sipping tea and eating cookies on the rocks ..."

Chapter Seven

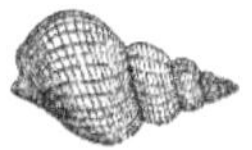

Chelsea spent most of Wednesday in the kitchen at The Salty Cupcake. Baking was soothing, but it didn't jar any memories for her. She was getting nowhere fast.

A quick trip to the hospital to see Jocelyn gave her no new perspectives. She was stuck. Jocelyn was stuck. She held her sister's hand without speaking for almost an hour, her frustration seething inside. She leaned toward crying, then toward screaming. She laid her head on her sister's shoulder and just breathed with her to calm down and then left.

Chelsea fielded several texts from her relatives all asking how she was, when Jocelyn was coming home, and if she needed anything. Enough! When she got Karsyn off the bus, she felt haggard and just wanted to read to her, snuggle, and block out the world. "Let's just sit on the couch together for a bit. What book do you want to read?"

"*Carrots for Harriet*!" Karsyn said. "Do the voices!"

A long pause. "I don't really remember them, but I'll give it a shot," Chelsea said.

Karsyn tipped her head and looked deep into Chelsea's eyes, almost like she was looking through her.

"Or I can just read it normal if you like …" Chelsea said. She crossed her arms and returned Karsyn's gaze, unsure of whether she should ask if something was wrong. It felt like she was being studied, and she wasn't in the mood. "I'm still having trouble remembering things, cupcake."

"I know, Mommy. It's OK. Just do what feels right to you," Karsyn answered.

"That was a big girl response." Chelsea grinned.

"I always give big girls reb-lonses," Karsyn quipped.

The two settled on the couch with *Carrots for Harriet*, and Chelsea began reading. On page three, it felt right to give one of the rabbits a deep, gruff voice. "'If you buy all the carrots, I won't be able to buy any,' grumbled Sam." *That was pretty good.*

"That's not Sam!" Karsyn interrupted.

"How does he talk?" Chelsea asked.

Again, Karsyn stared at her suspiciously. "He sounds like he's pinching his nose." She grabbed her nose as she spoke.

"OK. Take two. 'If you buy all the carrots, I won't be able to buy any,' grumbled Sam." Chelsea spoke in a nasal, snooty tone this time.

Karsyn fell over laughing. "That was wrong like backwards underwear!"

Cracking up, Chelsea threw her head back against the couch. "Oh, I give up!"

A short time later, Karsyn was packed to spend the night with her dad so Chelsea could have dinner with Julian. Damon rang the doorbell, and Karsyn raced down the stairs to answer it with Chelsea following behind at a normal pace.

"Doing OK, Chelse?"

"Much better today, but still low on memory." She raised her eyebrows, emphasizing the struggle. "Joss is about the same, but they have removed a lot of the bandages around her face. Swelling is going down, so she at least looks like she's healing."

"That's good. I'm glad to hear that."

Chelsea nibbled her lip as she watched Karsyn put her shoes on.

"Are you OK?" Damon asked.

Blinking, Chelsea forced a smile. "Yeah, I'm fine. Why?"

"You look nervous," Damon said. "Do you remember the *friend* you're having dinner with?" His emphasis on "friend" told her that he knew she was meeting a man.

"Honestly, I don't. But apparently, we were close before. We will see." Maybe she said too much.

"Bye, Mommy! See you tomorrow!" Karsyn threw her arms around Chelsea's legs.

Chelsea bent down and kissed her cheek, relishing the feeling of touching her skin. *This is my anchor.* "See you, love." *And I'll be OK tonight by myself without my anchor. She's in my heart.*

At the top of the stairs, in the kitchen, Chelsea saw the piece of sea glass that she found yesterday sitting on the counter. She picked it up and rubbed it with her thumb as she went back to her room to get ready.

"Now which dress says, 'I'm at a nice restaurant eating dinner with my boyfriend who I don't remember so don't get any ideas'?" A dilemma she never imagined she would be in. She finally chose a green dress with a pattern of pink ribbons and white pearls chasing down it. *Fun but appropriate for meeting a "friend."*

As she waited for Julian to pick her up, Chelsea paced the living room looking at a framed picture of Jocelyn and her in Florence. *Get better soon, sis.* She sent love to her sister and almost wished she were the one in the hospital bed right now as her hands started sweating again. The doorbell rang. Her stomach jumped.

When Chelsea answered the door, Julian kissed her on the cheek. "It's good to see you." He stepped back and looked at her for a moment. "You look beautiful. I thought we could go to The Captain's House since it's usually quiet on weeknights. That way we can just talk."

"That sounds good. I haven't been there in ages." Chelsea smiled nervously and wiped her hands on the side of her dress casually. Julian seemed nice, and he was definitely handsome.

Julian smiled politely at her. "We ate there a couple weeks ago. Don't worry about it. I'm sure all your memories will come back." He took her hand and led her to the car.

Inside the restaurant, Chelsea did her best not to make this feel like a first date, but she had to ask some questions to try to get her bearings. After drinks were ordered, she started with the obvious one. "So what do you do?"

Julian chuckled. "This is going to be fun. So, I started out doing graphic and web design and eventually started my own firm. I own OmniDigital Design on the mainland. We have contracts with a lot of major businesses on the East Coast, handling their social media presence, websites, and other online pieces that run in the background of their business."

"Oh, that sounds really interesting!" Chelsea said. It was a genuine response. "Do you work with influencers?"

"Not much. It's mostly brick and mortar. Lots of law firms. Some medical groups."

"Ah, I thought it would be flashier."

"This is why you once said you couldn't imagine doing the work I do. It was your nice way of saying that it's boring." Julian laughed again.

The server came over to take their order then.

"I'll have the seared red snapper please," Chelsea said. It came with peach chutney, jasmine rice, and grilled asparagus. "Do you have anything like mango lassi? I think that would be amazing with this."

"That *would* be great with this!" the server said. "We have a mango and cream martini?"

"Perfect," Chelsea said.

After Julian placed his order, the server left. Chelsea sipped her water while she waited on the martini.

"Into Indian food now?" Julian said.

"It sounded good. Exotic."

"I think you got hit harder than you thought. You've never been one for 'exotic.' You had chicken, veggies, and angel hair pasta last time we were here."

Chelsea made a face. "Well, I guess I'm going to be adventurous now! I really have no explanation for this."

"It's a good change. I love seeing you try new things."

"Well, right now, everything seems new."

Julian nodded and gave her a concerned smile. "Tell me about some of these new things. What's your world like right now?"

"I can navigate to the hospital and The Salty Cupcake without my phone, so there's a start. And I re-met Samantha and some of my employees. They've all been great. Really helpful. They are all understanding of my situation."

"That's good. So you didn't remember Sam either?"

"No. But she jumped right in and guided me on what we usually do. As it turns out, I do remember how to bake. From scratch! All the recipes I've tried are good. I guess some of my long-term memory is intact because these are recipes Joss and I made with our grandmother growing up. Sorry I'm rambling."

Julian smiled sweetly. "That's a start. But do you remember my favorite treat?"

Chelsea laughed uncomfortably and then paused. Then she said the first thing that came to mind. "Cinnamon biscotti?" Her face flushed as she instantly recalled that this is what Adrian had ordered when he came in the bakery. *Oops!*

Julian didn't seem to notice her embarrassment. "It's your coffee cake. There's cinnamon in it, so we will say you were close."

Chelsea chuckled nervously. "That's actually one of my favorites too. The sour cream really makes it. So, what do you like to do when you're not handling web stuff? I need to get to know you again."

"That stuff is top secret. I can't talk about it." Julian lightly lifted his hands off the table like he was pushing away the subject. They both laughed. "Actually, I used to party a lot when I was younger, but the past few years, I've been more into a good book, a great conversation, a small gathering of friends, a stroll on the beach. That sort of stuff. I like quiet, peace, and comfort."

"I feel all of that." Chelsea agreed. Maybe this wouldn't be so bad after all. "What about travel?"

"Not sure about India, but I've always want to go to Ireland and Scotland," Julian leaned forward and looked distant. "I didn't grow up with much, so we mostly came to the local beach or went camping in the woods. I've done that as I got older, but now I'm looking into exploring some, especially in countries where I already know the language." He chuckled. "In fact, that's something we were talking about before the accident."

"We were?" Chelsea bit her lip. *So, this was pretty serious.*

"Yeah. We were talking about our future, and I suggested taking a trip this fall. Together."

Instantly, Chelsea's throat tightened. "Our future?"

"Forget I said it. We will come back to it naturally, later, when you remember more."

"Thank you."

"Do you remember the nonprofit my company is starting? I know you loved talking about that before."

Furrowing her eyebrows, Chelsea gazed across the room for a moment. "I don't remember."

"I want to give back to the community by offering training to kids with computer talent in underprivileged communities. We're going to start teaching them how to build websites. There's an opportunity for mentorship, internships, and maybe even a job with us in the future. I'm still working on the plan and getting everything lined up, but it looks good. I'm pretty excited about it."

Chelsea let out a long deep breath. "I love that!"

Dinner was nice. The food was good. And the conversation with Julian was really pleasant. *He's a good listener, though we've talked mostly about him. That was necessary though. He seems to genuinely care about me. But I just feel ... numb. Scared?* Her thoughts flipped back to the man who kept coming up in her memories, and she forcefully shoved him aside.

Chelsea sipped the last of her mango cream martini. Exotic indeed. *Soooo good!* As nice as her dinner companion was, she felt like packing her bags and heading off to a foreign country as fast as possible.

A memory surfaced. She was in a hotel room in Italy. Not sure which city. Her sister was beside her. They started unpacking into the dressers in their shared room. She approached the window, cranked it open, and listened to the accordion player below.

"There is a market nearby. Let's go grab some fruit. I really want a mango, but that's a little impractical for walking around."

"I've heard they have nectarines the size of your head," her sister laughed.

"Then let's get those!" She threw her arms around Joss. "I'm so glad you're—"

"Thinking about something?" Julian interjected. He touched her hand and looked at her like she was his whole world, stars, and beyond. Chelsea jumped.

She forced herself to let him but really wanted to recoil. *There's no spark.* "I just thought of something my sister said."

Julian sat back. "I know it's hard with her in the hospital. Did you want to go see her? We could go together." When she hesitated, he went on. "I know you wanted me to meet her, so maybe you want to wait …"

"Let's wait," Chelsea said. "I'd rather you guys meet when she's better." She caught herself almost saying "if." *It hasn't been that long. She'll pull through.*

"Totally understand." Julian stood to leave and took her hand to help her up. "Do you want to watch a movie? We can just go back to your place and relax if you want. Or I can drop you off. Whatever you need right now, I'm here for you."

"I appreciate that," Chelsea said. She smiled. *He really does care.* "Let's do the movie. I've been wearing out early since the accident. I just want to relax." Then she added to be kind, "And I'd like you there too."

A short time later, they settled on the couch in Chelsea's living room and turned on a movie, Chelsea's pick. It was a light-hearted romance with minimal plot, so it would give her time to think, see if there was a spark as they sat together, and honestly rest. She was tired, both emotionally and physically.

As the movie started, Julian looked at Chelsea. "Are you sure you want me here? You don't look comfortable."

Chelsea realized she was frowning. "I'm fine. Really. Yes, please stay."

He wrapped an arm around her. "OK. If you change your mind, please just let me know. Really. It won't hurt my feelings. You've been through a lot."

Chelsea settled in against his side and leaned her head against his shoulder. He was muscular, handsome, nice to talk to. But this twinge in her gut told her to be careful. She realized that she had been shallow breathing all evening and focused on relaxing her breath.

Her mind drifted back to that boy who made her want to run. Who was he? What was that memory? And how long ago?

And even more so ... did she ever run? Or did she just keep pressing that feeling down?

Is that why she was feeling it now?

Chapter Eight

Zara was there again.

In the corner of Chelsea's bedroom, Zara stood silently till Chelsea sat up in her dream.

Again, she pointed at the mirror, then back to Chelsea.

Chelsea shook her head. "I don't understand. Can you help me? Can you tell me a different way?"

Zara nodded. She reached out for Chelsea. Her hand felt like a wisp of smoke, but Chelsea somehow took hold. Holding her hand felt like right before you touch an electric toothbrush, like the air was vibrating rapidly. She felt the feeling of love rush through her from her hand to her toes. The feeling of someone who is always there for you. The feeling of trust and hope.

Is that what it's like to be a spirit guide? Is that the other side?

Zara looked like she read Chelsea's thoughts. She touched her heart and then touched Chelsea's cheek with her other hand.

Chelsea shivered.

Then Zara beckoned for Chelsea to come with her. She rose from the bed and began to walk.

It felt like something shifted, and suddenly the women were in a dark room. A dim light in the corner showed someone in a bed.

"Jocelyn." Chelsea rushed to her side. Her heart fell as a terrible thought overtook her. "Zara, is she dying?"

Zara shook her head. She pointed at Jocelyn.

Chelsea placed her hand on Jocelyn's cheek. Jocelyn took a deep breath.

"Does she know I'm here?" she said excitedly. Zara nodded. "She senses me."

A short gasp came from the bed. Chelsea turned to look at Zara.

Beside her stood Jocelyn.

"No, no no no no no." Chelsea reached out to touch the wispy Jocelyn beside her, who looked confused.

Jocelyn stared at her arms and then turned to the two women before her. Diving, she raced back to the bed and touched her real arm.

Zara placed her hands on her cheeks and looked skyward. She shook her head.

Suddenly, Chelsea had a realization. "Hey, you're fine. Zara just wanted me to come see you. I've missed you. I hope you heal quickly. The doctors say you're getting better every day."

Jocelyn nodded. "Is Karsyn OK?"

"She's great. She misses you too. We're figuring things out together. I'm having a lot of trouble remembering."

"Me too," Jocelyn said. "I don't know if it's day or night. I don't know how many days have passed. I just sleep and talk to the Universe."

"Don't get too used to that. We need you here." Chelsea wiped a tear from her face. "It's almost been a whole week. Our birthday is the week after next. Promise me you'll at least be awake by then."

Jocelyn looked at the body lying in the bed. "I will do everything I can. I think this one is out of my hands though."

Chelsea grabbed her sister's apparition and held her. "Whatever you do, don't let go."

The room swayed. And suddenly, all three of them were bobbing along over an open plain.

"Where are we?" Chelsea said. She swung her head right and left and couldn't believe what she saw. Zara and Jocelyn were flanking her, riding on elephants. Jocelyn still wore her hospital gown.

"I love elephants," Jocelyn whispered. "I've never ridden one."

"You have," Chelsea said. "Karsyn and I were talking about the video of you on the elephant. It was amazing."

"I don't remember," Jocelyn said. "That's concussions for you."

"It will come back. Mine is starting to."

"I need you to remember," Jocelyn said.

As suddenly as the elephants appeared, they were gone, and Chelsea was alone in her bedroom again with Zara.

"Zara, thank you for taking me to Jocelyn."

Zara placed her hands over her heart and then pointed at the mirror again.

"I'm becoming more myself every day. So is she." Chelsea smiled, certain that she figured out Zara's message.

Zara sighed and then looked up and shook her head, but Chelsea didn't notice.

"Mommy," a tiny voice said. "Mommy, there's an elephant in my room making noise."

Chelsea sat up with a start, gasping for air. *I was wrong. Something is wrong. Zara was trying to tell me.* "I'm sure it's OK. Let's just go see." Her calm voice muffled the pounding of her heart.

Together, the two walked across the room. Karsyn had a death grip on Chelsea's hand. As Chelsea approached, she heard a distinct but muffled bugling sound. And she had no logical explanation for it.

Karsyn trembled and pointed at the closet. She remained in the doorway as Chelsea entered the room.

Of course, it's in the closet. She shuddered and flicked on the bedroom light, blinding herself. *Mamas have to be brave.* Softly, she padded across the floor and pulled the closet door open, gritting her teeth. The sound emanated from a pile of toys on the floor.

Cautiously, Chelsea picked through the toys, getting closer and closer to the source of the sound. Then, there it was: a toy elephant resting on a button that produced the trumpeting sound. The battery must have been low because it was soft and eerie.

I didn't hear this earlier. How did it start in the middle of the night? Chelsea scooped up the toy. "Here it is, baby. It really was an elephant." She set it on the nightstand.

"I don't want it in my room." Karsyn looked shaken.

And I don't blame you. "I'll take it downstairs. Good night, lovey." Chelsea kissed her daughter and tucked her back in bed. Karsyn was out in seconds. Then, Chelsea picked up the elephant and walked down to the living room with it.

"Now how am I supposed to get back to sleep with a possessed elephant in my house?" Chelsea sat on the couch for a moment and suddenly felt like someone was in the room with her. She looked around. "Karsyn?" Definitely not. She shuddered. And then she realized it was Zara. *Something about elephants, huh?*

She closed her eyes for a minute and tried to tune in, in case she was supposed to hear a message, but nothing came through. Then, she walked out on the balcony off of the living room, facing the ocean. The sound was crisp and true, though a little distant. It seemed like an old friend. *You're always here for me. Just like Zara.*

How many times in my life has Zara signaled to me that something was wrong? Usually, she sends a butterfly. If she's sending an elephant ... it must be a larger-than-life issue.

So where was the butterfly when I was about to hit that truck and send Jocelyn into a coma?

"It was for your greatest and highest good." Zara's answer came through crystal clear.

Chelsea fumed and flipped a bird at the night sky. "That's what I think of your 'greatest and highest good' bullshit, Universe. You could have let Zara send a butterfly. Or a nudge."

A memory suddenly came floating to the surface.

When Chelsea was in Spain, she met the most amazing man. They both spoke fluent Spanish to each other till they realized neither of them were from there. He was from Canada, of all places, but his family was from Spain, so he looked Spanish. Her hair was dark brown at the time, so she could pull off being a local, especially when she spoke.

After hanging out all evening, they went back to her hostel and up to the roof to talk and look at the city.

"Of all the places to meet you, it's halfway around the world. And on my last night in town," he said in English.

"Better make the moment last then," she chuckled.

He cupped her chin and gazed into her eyes for a moment. Then he kissed her as if they had known each other a thousand years.

She wrapped her arms around him and ran a hand through his tousled curls. He pulled her tight against him, arms caressing her back, one hand moving down to her waist.

Leaning back, she pulled her face away to gaze at him a moment, figuring out where this was going, when she noticed a butterfly painted on the wall.

She froze.

That was when several other people from the hostel came up on the roof. They were laughing, talking loudly, and crowding around a young woman with a bag in her hands. Probably drugs.

Chelsea caught her breath and pulled him with her toward the stairs, glad she had chosen that moment to step back into reality. Shaking off their excitement, the pair just went for a walk, holding hands and enjoying a few more lingering kisses along the way before he had to go back to his hotel. His flight home left early in the morning.

Why was I in Spain? And when? It doesn't seem that long ago ... but I was clearly not there with Damon.

"God, who am I?" Chelsea shook her head and stared at the space between buildings that just gave her a glimpse of the ocean with pale moonlight glistening on the water. She stared a moment longer till her eyelids drooped, and she determined that it was time to return to bed, hopefully for a little more sleep.

In the morning, she was groggy. "Weird sleep and mid-thirties don't mix," Chelsea muttered as she climbed from bed. "And Joss needs me to remember." She picked a beachy sundress, denim jacket, and sandals and hurried through the morning routine with Karsyn.

When she arrived at The Salty Cupcake, she parked and dragged herself through the door.

"Happy Thursday morning! How's my favorite cupcake rockstar?" Samantha said. She greeted her with a half hug as she danced around her with a tray of scones. "You need coffee. I just made some."

"Thank you! I don't know how you do it with three littles. I've only got one." Chelsea grabbed a cup and filled it with a dark roast. Then she splashed in almond milk and a little sugar.

"Why did Karsyn have you up last night? Is she sick?"

Chelsea stirred her coffee and made a bitter face. "An elephant started making noise in the middle of the night. I shut it off. It was pretty bizarre because I was just dreaming about riding an elephant."

"That sounds like a sign to me."

Chelsea rolled her eyes and yawned. "Are you into that stuff?"

"I've been 'seeing things' since I was a kid. And I do yoga … meditate … Reiki. So yeah, I'm into that stuff."

"Then I need to tell you about this."

Chelsea filled Samantha in on the dream with Zara last night.

"This is the first time I've heard about Zara."

"I never mentioned her before?"

"No. I wonder why …"

"I can't imagine. She's been a normal part of my life and Jocelyn's since we were really little. I actually can't remember a time without Zara. She grew up with us."

"Does she only show up to warn you about things?"

"Not always. Sometimes she sends a butterfly to warn us. And sometimes when she shows up, she's just connecting with us, pointing us in the right direction. We've learned to communicate with her as we all grew up. She's kind of a guardian for us."

"What do you mean 'as you all grew up'? If she's a spirit, then she would stay the same age … wouldn't she?"

"As Joss and I got older, Zara got older with us. She's always the same age as us. When we were little, she was little. Now she's an adult."

"That's strange that she grew with you. I always thought that a guardian angel was an adult. Are you sure she doesn't mean trouble for you? What if she's a spirit that has latched onto you and is sucking your energy? Can they do that your whole life? Should we go see someone about this?"

"Oh, no. I don't think I was clear about this. Samantha, she's my sister."

Chapter Nine

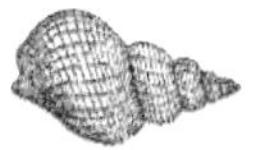

"You never told me you had another sister."

"I guess the subject never came up. It's not something I talk about a lot." Chelsea sipped her coffee. "We were triplets, but she died at birth. So, we've just always been deeply connected."

"That makes a lot more sense now. So, she's always the same age as you. Does she look like you?"

"Yes, she's identical. If you saw the three of us together, it would be hard to tell us apart."

"That's amazing …"

Chelsea nodded, her eyes clouded with tears. *What would happen if I lost Joss too?* Then, her phone buzzed in her pocket. Tipping her head back, she blinked and took a deep breath before answering it. Samantha skittered through the door into the restaurant with the scones.

She didn't recognize the number. "Hello?"

"Hi … Jocelyn?"

"No, this is her sister."

"Oh. You two sound alike. I'm looking for her. This is the emergency number she listed in her contacts."

"I see. And who is this?"

"Amber Baumgardner. I'm with Alles Deutch. Jocelyn was supposed to confirm our schedule for an upcoming promotion we were doing with her and her show."

"Oh."

"Do you know her schedule? We have a deal with a local network, too, and we wanted to get her some time on one of the shows."

"Wow, I'm sure she will love that." Chelsea felt her heart in her throat. "I can't give you any information, though. She was in a car accident, and she's still in the hospital."

"I'm sorry to hear that. Could you ask her to call me then?"

"I can ... but I'm not sure when that will be. She's been in a coma for almost a week now."

Amber gasped. "I'm so sorry to hear that. I certainly hope she's better soon. Is it OK with you if I convey this to our team? We need to plan a work-around in case she's delayed."

"It's OK with me. I know she was really excited about this trip. I wish I could give you better information, but everything is up in the air." Her voice sounded steady, but she felt strained.

"I understand. Please give her my best, and I hope she has a speedy recovery. We will talk with her soon."

After hanging up, Chelsea felt a panic rising. *I need to save this for her. Maybe I can go in her place.* And moments later she realized that wasn't even possible. *I can't just jump on a plane and try to be her. I don't know what she does. I barely know what I do.*

She slid her phone back into her pocket. *How am I supposed to navigate this?*

"One step at a time," a voice said.

But I don't even know what direction to step in half the time ...

Pushing the door open, Chelsea joined Samantha behind the counter. When Samantha looked at her, Chelsea just sighed.

"Do you want to talk about it?" Samantha looked concerned.

"It was a call for Joss. The company she was supposed to work with in Germany was looking for her. I had to let them know what happened."

"I see." Samantha threw her hands in the air. "There just isn't much you can do about that till she's better."

"I just wish she would wake up. At least then—"

The door jingled, and Adrian walked in.

Chelsea's face reddened as she looked at him, just walking like a normal human being into a coffee and pastry shop for his morning fix. Butterflies fluttered from her stomach to her toes and then up to her brain. Then, because it was apparently empty in there since the accident, the butterflies stayed in her head.

"You're staring," Samantha hissed.

Inhaling deeply, Chelsea glanced into the case nonchalantly. "Should I grab anything from the back?"

Smirking, Samantha replied, "No, I think we're good for now. Hi, Adrian."

"Good morning. Morning Chelsea. How are you?"

"Good. I'm good. I'm doing … good." She placed an elbow on the case and told the butterflies to stop it.

"I'll get your usual," Samantha offered.

"Thanks. So, Chelsea, how's your sister?"

"Not much difference. I stopped in yesterday and talked to her. I brought photo albums. I thought maybe she would respond to all my talking and reminiscing, but nothing happened."

"That's too bad. Are you guys pretty close?"

"We are. We always have been. She travels a lot though, so I usually have to keep up with her on her blog or social media. Joss's Journeys has been a big focus for her for the last eight years, and it's gotten pretty big, to the point where she launched her show *Braving Borders*. She was supposed to go to Germany next to film and connect with some companies there about … some stuff." Chelsea was suddenly very self-conscious. "I'm sorry if I'm rambling."

Adrian smiled. It was adorable and mischievous, with a dimple on his left cheek. His eyes danced as they looked at her. "I don't mind. We haven't had a chance to talk other than greeting each other and you handing me my coffee."

"I've had a lot on my mind lately. I guess it's just spilling out." Her eye twitched, betraying the chaos brewing inside.

"No doubt. That was a pretty big event." Adrian picked up the cup that Samantha was silently offering him. "So, you said her blog is Joss's Journey? I have actually read some of her stuff and watched *Braving Borders*. I couldn't put my finger on why she looked so familiar. But her hair is different from yours, so that's probably why."

"Right …"

"So, have you been able to travel with her? It looks like she has some amazing adventures."

"I have! I went to Tuscany with her last year. It was gorgeous. We hit Florence and some of the smaller towns nearby. A vineyard. I think it's the longest we've spent together in a long time."

"That sounds nice. I went to Rome a few years ago. I did some city hopping, spending a few days here and there. I didn't get to see Florence though. What did you like there?"

"The Ponte Vecchio was lovely. It's so old and yet bustling. It's a super old bridge that's lined with shops selling all sorts of things. Just fascinating. Plus, the view up and down the river. We ate house-made ravioli at a little restaurant near there and just people-watched …" Chelsea's face softened as she talked about it. *It's weird how fresh this memory is. Like it was bubbling under the surface just waiting to be discovered.*

"You really lit up talking about it. You must have loved it." Adrian said gently. He smiled again and sipped his coffee. "Hey, I have to go. I have a client in twenty. But it was great talking to you today. I'll see you tomorrow." He scooped up his biscotti from the counter.

"See ya!" Chelsea called. She did a little finger wave and then spun on her heel and started toward the door to the kitchen.

OK, the finger wave was a little weird, but that conversation felt so good. It was like time stood still when we talked. And all I noticed was how his amber-brown eyes were locked on me. I feel like I can breathe again, like that gave me a little lift.

"Whaaat was that?" Samantha said. She had followed Chelsea into the kitchen without her noticing. Three other employees were busy at a table at the back cutting up a cake and plating some treats.

Chelsea raised her eyebrows. "What?"

"You have *never* shown any interest in him before," Samantha started, "and now, every time he walks in, it's like you're tripping over yourself." Chelsea couldn't hide her smile. "And what's with the little finger wave?"

Chelsea sighed and wrinkled her nose.

"If I didn't know you just got hit with a truck, I'd think someone unplugged you and rebooted your whole system."

"Yeah, I'll be honest. That was weird." Chelsea chuckled. "But everything else was so nice. I enjoyed talking to him."

"Not to put a damper on your mood, because I'm really liking the 'dancing on a cloud' thing you're doing, but ... have you talked to Julian?" Samantha gave her a serious look.

Suddenly back on earth, Chelsea turned and pulled some ingredients out of the cupboard. "I did. We had dinner Wednesday and watched a movie at my place."

"You don't sound excited about it."

Measuring the flour, Chelsea grimaced. "I honestly wasn't. It was fine." She looked back at Samantha. "I don't know."

A concerned look crossed Samantha's face. She took a gentle tone. "Chelse, you guys were pretty serious before the accident. I don't want you to throw it away without some consideration. You're my best friend. I care about you."

"I'm not throwing it away." She frowned and creamed the sugar with butter. Then she added the eggs and vanilla. When she was done mixing, she turned to Samantha, who was still standing there. "Look, I appreciate you looking out for me. And I know I've been confused and mixed up since the accident. I'm taking things slowly. And I won't do anything rash."

"Promise?"

"I promise."

"Julian was really important to you before. You guys were talking about a future. I know that we change every day, we learn and grow. Sometimes the Universe throws a curveball our way, but when we know our path deep in our hearts, we don't waver. Trust yourself. Trust your heart. But take your time too."

Chelsea grabbed Samantha's hand. "Thank you. I needed that." A tear ran down her cheek.

When the sugar cookies came out of the oven, Chelsea breathed in deeply. The scent was like nothing else. It reminded her of growing up in her grandmother's kitchen. It's what home and love and deep trust smell like.

Inhaling the sweetness of the cookies, Chelsea stared at them as they cooled. Funny how every time she steps in the kitchen, it's like everything is back to normal. The recipes come. The sweets get baked. And life is good. In the kitchen, there are no worries.

She grabbed a spatula and placed all the cookies on the cooling racks. Shortly after, Chelsea drove to the hospital again to see Jocelyn.

"I dreamed about Zara last night, sis. And you. We were right here, talking. It felt so real. I know Zara wanted to tell me something." Chelsea took hold of Jocelyn's hand and stroked the back of it. "I still don't remember much from before. I met Julian last night and had dinner with him. It was ... weird. I don't remember anything about him. It's like I was hanging out with a stranger. He's nice, but I don't know if I love him. I don't know ... so much."

A nurse came in to check on Jocelyn and then left the room again.

"And no one except Samantha knew about him because I didn't want Karsyn to know yet. I was protecting her. It makes sense, but it's about the only thing that makes sense!" She squeezed her eyes shut as they welled up with tears again. "All I know is how much I love you and miss you ... God, Joss, I wish you could wake up. I wish I could remember for you!"

Chelsea's legs were feeling wobbly again, disconnected. The desire to run trembled through her. She needed to escape. Reality couldn't hold her in place. She was uncomfortable, so she had to get out. Now. Shaking, she placed her forehead against the back of Jocelyn's hand and let the tears flow. She closed her eyes.

Breathe in. Breathe out.

A moment later, she opened her purse and pulled a tissue out. The little elephant keychain swung joyfully from the zipper as she wiped her tears and blew her nose as quietly as she could. She was always self-conscious of her emotions.

"I have to go get Karsyn, Joss. But I want to leave you this." She pulled the chunk of sea glass that she found at the beach with Karsyn from her purse and placed it on the nightstand. "Sea glass is for renewal and healing. I know you need this. Get better. I love you."

Another memory glinted in her mind, and she snatched at it, digging in like she was pulling piles of sand away from a treasure. Jocelyn was there. "I want you to have this. It's for renewal and healing. After Vic, you need to step back and heal yourself. You know I've always been beside you, and I didn't believe all the lies he told us. I knew he was hurting you. I could see it in the way you carried yourself. You were shrinking. But you can heal now. And I'm with you."

Chelsea held out her hands, and Jocelyn gave her an enormous piece of sea glass. Even in the memory, she could still feel the weight of it. "Thank you," she sobbed. Then the sisters wrapped their arms around each other.

"I'm here. Whatever you need, just tell me," Jocelyn said.

The memory faded away, and Chelsea was back in the hospital room. "Vic. So that was his name." She saw the shaggy teen with his sneer in her mind's eye and wondered what she ever saw in that guy. Then she shook the thought from her head and focused on the message. *The sea glass in the meditation ... was I supposed to leave it at the hospital? Or was I just supposed to leave a piece, and it didn't matter which one?* "Or am I missing the message altogether?" she mumbled. "Signs are so confusing."

Suddenly, she got an idea. "Didn't I see a therapist after the divorce? I wonder if that would help me remember ... now what was her name?" She stared at her phone a moment. Then, she searched. "What would I have her listed as? Shrink? Head doc? Therapist?"

When she typed "therapist," a name actually popped up. "How normal. Why did I list her like that? Dr. Annie Harper, I am giving you a call. Let's see what we can dredge up and pick up life where we left off ..."

Chapter Ten

The next day, much to her relief, Julian only texted a couple times and called her for a few minutes Friday evening.

I didn't mind spending time with him. He seems nice, like he would be interesting to talk to more often … but this is better till I can wrap my head around how I feel. How is it my heart is so empty right now? It's like the only normal feelings I have are around Karsyn.

The phone conversation with Julian was pleasant, but they seemed like two friends talking. He skirted any important topics like their relationship or the future … or even the past. And Chelsea just focused on work, Karsyn, and Jocelyn. *Sadly, this may be going nowhere, and he may start to feel it soon. How long is this guy going to be patient?*

Do I even care?

I guess it's only been a week.

In the back of her mind, Chelsea kept thinking about the elephant dream with Zara and Jocelyn. *There has to be a bigger meaning to it.*

Around lunchtime on Saturday, Chelsea took Karsyn with her to grab a treat at The Salty Cupcake.

After spending the past few nights at her dad's, Karsyn wanted to "go exploring" all day with Mommy, and Chelsea was only too happy to oblige. They skipped happily into the shop through the front door, and Karsyn immediately approached the case full of treats.

"I don't know you," she announced to the cashier. "What's your name?"

The cashier smiled at Karsyn and then at her mom. "Hi, I'm Kelli. I just started working here. What's your name?"

"Karsyn Beckett. I'm five, and I am actually part mermaid. That's why I have this sparkly purse."

"That's an awesome purse, Karsyn. Can I get you a treat?"

"Thank you! A Salty Cupcake special. Mommy, what would you like?"

"A mini-cini-roll. And a coffee," Chelsea said.

"Got it," Kelli said. "Your daughter is so cute."

"Thank you!"

Just then, Samantha waved from the doorway to the kitchen. "Hey ladies, it's been a long time!"

"I thought you were off today," Chelsea said.

"No, just yesterday," Samantha answered.

"I thought ... geez, I don't know," Chelsea laughed. "I can't keep this straight yet."

"No worries ... you're not worried, are you?" Samantha laughed. "You know I have things under control here."

"I'm not. It's just the whole, well everything ... Life." Chelsea slumped as she thought about it and then forcefully pressed her shoulders back.

Samantha handed her a coffee. "I know. It's bound to get better. Any change with Joss?"

"No, and I keep thinking about … stuff." Chelsea stared at Karsyn's cupcake—a salted caramel cupcake with chocolate chips and a chocolate mermaid tail. "So that's a 'Salty Cupcake special'?" She handed it to Karsyn, who immediately grabbed it and ran to a table. "I'll be right there, hon."

"What sort of stuff? Any interesting dreams?"

"I had one a few days ago about Zara, Jocelyn, and me riding elephants."

"That's bizarre."

"I know. I don't know what it's supposed to mean."

"Well, elephants are supposed to be guardians. Maybe she was just trying to tell you that you are both protected and safe. You tend to worry about Joss a lot, you know. Maybe Zara wanted you to feel comforted, especially now while Joss is in the hospital."

"That's a good point. She's just saying that she's looking out for us."

"That's what I think anyway."

"It makes sense."

"Did you bump into Adrian while I was out?" Samantha smiled slyly.

Suddenly, Chelsea felt a fire light inside of her. *Maybe I'm not totally numb* … "I did. But he was in a hurry yesterday. Couldn't stop and talk."

"Oh well."

Chelsea shrugged. "I'm going to join Karsyn. I'll talk to you later." She smiled as she thought about the way Adrian had turned to look at her as he ran out the door to get to his meeting. That smile ...

After their treats, Chelsea and Karsyn drove to the hospital to see Jocelyn.

"I miss Aunt Joss," Karsyn said. "I wish she was OK. I was excited to play with her while she was here."

"I know," Chelsea said. Her voice quavered and she gripped the seam on her shirt tightly. She couldn't help but think that the longer Jocelyn was in a coma, the slimmer her chance was of coming out of it. "Was there something special you wanted to do with her?"

"Mommy. I already told you."

"I'm sorry if I forgot. I'm still having trouble with my memories."

Karsyn frowned and stomped her foot. "You keep forgetting me! I just wanted to build sandcastles and race on the beach and play dolls and make s'mores around the fire pit and have birthday cake with her."

Chelsea whispered, "Is that all?" Wow, she felt guilty.

"No. I'll ask what else she wanted to do because I'm a good host." Karsyn crossed her arms and glared at her mother.

"You're sweet, baby. I'm sure, when she wakes up, she will be so excited to start on that list with you."

"I want her to take me to ride on an elephant."

"Me too, baby. Me too."

When they walked in Jocelyn's room, Chelsea set a small vase of wildflowers on the table, while Karsyn raced to hug Jocelyn.

"Maybe Zara sent those elephants to say we have guardians," Chelsea whispered as she touched Jocelyn's hair. She noticed that after not being washed for several days, her normally beautiful hair had dulled and lay flat on the pillow. Brushing it away from Jocelyn's face, she saw that the cut on her forehead was healing well, and the bruising had faded to a sickly yellow. Aside from the injuries, she appeared peaceful, like she was dreaming.

At that moment, Chelsea realized that Karsyn was looking at her strangely. "Everything OK?"

Karsyn turned back to Jocelyn and hugged her tightly, but her face revealed that the gears in her little head were spinning.

"Karsyn, I know you're upset because I keep forgetting. Is something else wrong? You need to tell me if you know something." Panicked, Chelsea looked at all the monitors around Jocelyn. Nothing clued her in to a problem, not that she really knew what to look for.

"Aunt Joss just smells ... different."

Frowning, Chelsea looked back at Karsyn. "The nurses are helping to wash her. Maybe it's the soap they are using. It's probably different from what she usually uses."

The little girl hugged her aunt again. She shook her head. "No, Mommy. She smells like you."

Leaning down, Chelsea hugged her sister. As her nose brushed Jocelyn's hair, she caught the faintest scent of perfume. The same perfume she had just put on that morning.

"It's funny. I think we wear the same perfume," Chelsea said. She didn't think much of it, though. *Aren't twins supposed to be closer than most sisters? It's possible that they would randomly pick the same perfume.*

Karsyn's eyes penetrated Chelsea, like she was trying to stare into her soul. *What is this child thinking about?* Then she swiftly turned and gazed at Jocelyn the same way.

Chelsea cleared her throat. "Hey, tell Aunt Joss about school this week. Didn't you have a fun guest at your assembly?"

Karsyn lit up. "We did! She wrote a book about mermaids with her daughter ..." She rambled about the guest and her book, as Chelsea listened.

I wish Joss could respond to this. God, I hope she wakes up soon. I hope she's not relying on me to remember something special to get her out of this. A few minutes later, she could tell that Karsyn was winding down. She squeezed Jocelyn's hand. "Sis, we are going to head out, but I'll be back tomorrow to see you again. I love you." Kissing her cheek, she felt how warm her skin still felt. She was still full of life. "Come back to us!" she whispered.

Chelsea took Karsyn's hand and started across the room when suddenly the little girl slipped away and ran back to Jocelyn. She threw her arms around her and breathed in deeply. Chelsea watched as her daughter whispered, "I love you," and then ran back to her. Her eyes welled up with tears as she looked down at her little sweetheart. She blinked, and they spilled over.

Smiling, Karsyn met her gaze. "She needed another hug. Don't cry, Mommy." After another glance back at the woman in the bed, Karsyn grabbed Chelsea's hand and walked out the door with her.

Wiping away the tears with her other hand, Chelsea focused on her anchor, walking beside her and slowed her breathing. It was weird how warm she felt when she held Karsyn's hand. Since the accident, every time they held hands, it was like she was noticing for the first time. Holding her hand felt like home in a sea of things that felt nothing like it.

* * *

Monday morning, Chelsea dropped Karsyn off at the bus and then went to the office of Annie Harper, MD, LCPC to try to untangle some of her past and kick start her memory. For Joss, just in case. She still had surprisingly huge gaps in memory, especially when it came to her relationship with Julian, as well as with Damon. She didn't remember much about her ex-husband at all. Of course, he spent a lot of time working, but she couldn't even recall the tender moments with him. It was so strange.

The waiting room at Dr. Harper's office was stylish and clean. All neutrals. *Nothing that would trigger anyone, I suppose. Keep everyone calm while they wait.*

She noted a black and white photo of the beach on one wall beside a black and white of a beautiful tree with fleeting clouds. Another black and white of a field of wildflowers on another wall. *Why would you have a black-and-white photo of wildflowers? Aren't the gorgeous colors the point?* Chelsea closed her eyes. She was fine. Everything was fine. She hoped Dr. Harper had answers for her.

"Chelsea," the receptionist called.

When she was seated across from the therapist's chair, she noted the calm in the office as well. The couch was firm but comfortable with pillows and a big fluffy blanket on one end. There was a vase of flowers on the desk, which provided a rare pop of color. The therapist entered a moment later.

"Ah, Chelsea. It's been a few weeks. What's new?"

"Dr. Harper, I—"

"Call me 'Annie'." She pursed her lips and crinkled an eyebrow.

"*Annie*, I was in an accident with my sister. You may have seen it on the news a few days ago. A truck hit us head on, and Jocelyn is in a coma. I am struggling with my memory but otherwise doing OK."

"I'm sorry to hear that. Sarah said your message mentioned needing help remembering something. How long ago did you say the accident was?"

"A little over a week. A week and a half."

"OK, sometimes it can take a while to get your memory back. The most important thing is patience and being gentle with yourself. Have you tried anything to spark those memories?"

"Mostly focusing on Karsyn and talking with her. Talking to Joss. Looking at things that seem to mean something to me to see if they bring back a memory. Walking on the beach. Photo albums. Baking. Meditating ..."

"Those are all really good things. Tell me more about meditating. Have you been able to relax and trigger any memories that way?"

"Not much."

"I would like you to keep doing that, even if it doesn't immediately bring you memories. Just getting your body into a state of calm should help lead it back to normalcy anyway, so you might notice little things coming back."

"Most of the things that pop into my head have been from movies, I think. They seem pretty exotic. A couple days ago, I was mediating, and I pictured myself in a Buddhist temple. It felt almost like I had been there before, but I can't imagine that I have. So, it was probably a movie, but I don't know what movie. It was really peaceful, though, so I stayed there for the meditation. It felt so grounded and tropical. I'd love to find out if it's a real place."

"That's very interesting. Usually, you picture a meadow when you meditate. I remember we talked about that before because you love the wildflowers you always see there."

"A meadow? I said that?" She recalled the wildflowers in the flower bed near her front door.

"You did. I had wildflowers on my desk that day, and you talked about them and how much you loved them, especially sweet peas."

Turning, Chelsea gazed at the flowers on the desk. She furrowed her brow, trying to recall this conversation. She shook her head. Something felt wrong. "I've been going to the beach in my meditations lately, except the day I was in a Buddhist temple, but that didn't feel weird either." *Maybe Annie got me mixed up with someone else.*

"Don't worry about it. It's possible that things have changed since we last talked, too." She made a note on her pad that reminded Chelsea that every word she said was potentially being analyzed. Her chest tightened as she wondered if she would end up on meds for her memory issues. Or her meditation habits.

"Speaking of ... the last time we talked was last month, after your miscarriage. How have you been coping with that?"

The silence in the room felt like lead.

Parting her lips, Chelsea tried to speak, but no words escaped. Her mouth was dry. She pursed her lips. Then she shook her head in disbelief. "I-did ... I—what? Miscarriage?" She put both hands over her heart.

Annie took her glasses off and gave her a look full of sympathy. "You weren't very far along, but you and Julian were excited to find out you were pregnant. Do you remember that part?"

Her head was spinning. Suddenly, the room felt too small.

"Chelsea, take a long, slow deep breath. Now let it out as I count to four. One ... two ... three ... four ... Let's do it again." She guided her through several more breaths.

Leaning forward, Chelsea put her head in her hands. *A baby? And I don't remember that?*

"Have you talked to Julian since the accident? When we talked before, you two were talking about your future together, making plans. The miscarriage was upsetting, but it didn't change things. Does that help? How does that feel?" She handed Chelsea a tissue, and Chelsea swabbed the corner of her eyes. She was still reeling.

"We've talked a few times, but he is trying to be gentle. He knows I don't remember much. Honestly, it's been really strange. I didn't even remember him— no, I *still* don't remember him!" Her anger started rising. "How can I possibly have been in a relationship with someone and not remember him after the accident? Worse, I was *pregnant with his child*? What kind of a person loses those types of memories? All I keep remembering is stuff from my childhood and stuff with Joss. Good grief!"

"Chelsea, don't judge yourself. You will remember. The childhood memories are a good start. It's OK. You can't control what you do and don't remember. When your brain is ready, it will recall those things."

Chelsea couldn't respond. She just stared straight ahead of her as her mind swirled.

"Let's try hypnosis. That has worked before."

"Um ... OK."

Annie asked her to sit comfortably and close her eyes. "Since you're used to the beach for meditation, let's go there now. I'd like you to listen to the waves crashing on the shore. Sit down and relax into the sand. What is it that you like about the beach?"

Chelsea pushed her agitation down and forced a smile. "It feels like family vacations when I was little. Joss and I would go with our parents. We always met up with my mom's family. Her sister Dana and her brother Eric, all my cousins. We loved playing in the sand and swimming all day. It feels like I have a lot of happy memories from that time."

"That's good. We want the warmth, the cozy feelings. I'm glad that your long-term memory is strong."

"Me too." Finally, something is going right.

"Now, let's imagine that Karsyn sits down beside you. What happens next?"

"She grabs me with both arms for a quick hug. Then she pulls my arms so I get up. She wants me to play in the sand with her."

"Very good. Now, someone else approaches you with a picnic basket. Who is coming to join you?"

Chelsea frowned. "It's a man wearing a beat-up flannel. He doesn't belong here. I don't feel like I want him near us. I suddenly want to run."

"Chelsea, you know you're safe here. You are in control. You can ask him to leave."

She paused. "He's leaving, but I feel sort of smashed down inside. I think I knew him before. I think I dated him ... maybe in high school." She didn't want to say much more. Pushing him from her memory was her only desire.

"OK, let's try something else. We don't want the negative stuff to overtake the good memories, especially if we aren't progressing to anything recent and important."

Chelsea's mind was still spinning when she left a short time later without any new answers. This whole other life that she doesn't even know about had washed ashore, and she felt stranded in the middle of what people tell her are her memories, wading through the confusion, waiting for her ship to come in.

Chapter Eleven

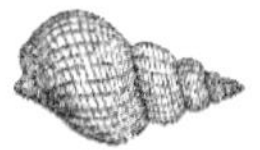

"Mommy, are you OK?" Karsyn asked. She snuggled against Chelsea on the couch that evening and handed her a stuffed unicorn with rainbow wings.

Shaking herself out of her reverie, Chelsea forced a weak smile. "I'm just tired, cupcake." *Mentally tired. From all the crazy things I'm learning about myself!*

After a night of tossing and turning, Chelsea was wide awake when her alarm gently prodded her from sleep with its harp song. It seemed that her brain just wouldn't shut off. She bit her lip. *A whole life that I didn't know about. Did something happen to cause the miscarriage? Did we plan the pregnancy? Probably not. That's awfully quick. Should I talk to Julian about this?*

Do I even want to talk to him?

Karsyn eyed her suspiciously as Chelsea mindlessly dunked and redunked her tea bag in her mug. "Mommy. Are you nervous?"

"No, baby, I'm OK. Really. It's just been a long week."

"It's Tuesday. Mommy, do you need a vacation?"

Chelsea laughed. "I think I do. Maybe the beach tonight?"

Clapping, Karsyn leaped from her chair, still holding her cereal spoon. "Yay yay yay! I want to build sandcastles and splash in the ocean!"

"Let's do it then! I'll take you there after school."

Throwing her arms around Chelsea, spoon still in hand, Karsyn sunk her face into Chelsea's hair. "I love you, Mommy."

Chelsea teared up and smiled. "I love you too, baby."

A short time later, Chelsea watched Karsyn get on the bus and then hopped in her car. She felt so much better physically since the accident, but her head was always a swarm of confusion, buzzing like bees around honey. When she pulled up outside of The Salty Cupcake, she sat in the car a few minutes and tried to regroup.

*Breathe, Chelse. We will figure it all out. Everything that happens to me happens **for** me, and I will overcome the challenges. I know I've got this.* "But crap, really, a baby with that guy?"

When she entered the kitchen, Chelsea went straight to the "Bake Me!" board, where she found a list of treats that they need for the day. She ran her finger over the list, determined to focus on something other than the craziness of her life. "I ... want ... a challenge. Ah, gluten-free chocolate doughnuts." She erased it from the board and set to work.

She tapped the screen on the tablet above the counter and typed in the recipe. When it popped up, she got started. Focusing on that recipe would surely keep her from drifting back into the "what ifs" and "what the hells" from her therapy session and the past few days of bizarre happenings.

Pouring. Mixing. Chelsea finished the batter, prepped the pan, and placed the doughnuts in the oven. She ran a finger through the bowl to taste the mix. Eh. A little potato-y, but not terrible. The glaze would help. As she waited for the oven to ding, she created the dairy-free drizzle, in keeping with the allergy sensitive theme, and dipped a spoon in to taste. Now THAT was good!

Staying busy in the kitchen, Chelsea managed to distract herself for a couple hours, focusing only on bake shop needs. Once the doughnuts had cooled, she poured the glaze over the top and then finished with a vanilla drizzle. Beautiful! And safe for people with allergies! If she could high-five herself, she would.

I wonder if I've made these before. Or maybe I had one of the girls make them ... They don't seem familiar ... Definitely not one of Grandma's recipes.

Close to eleven thirty a.m., she backed through the door into the restaurant with the tray of doughnuts, as well as a tray of sea salt caramel macarons that Maisie had been making.

As she gently slid the trays into place in the display, Chelsea sensed someone staring at her. She turned and then gasped. Right on the other side of the counter was Adrian.

"Good morning." He smiled that wide grin with the big dimple, and Chelsea had to remember to close her jaw. "You know, we have to stop meeting this way."

"Um, good morning. I didn't see you there. I was in my own world," she laughed.

"I could tell. Doing OK?"

I can hardly tell him about what's spinning in my head. "Yeah. Good. Just … thinking about my sister, you know. I'm worried is all."

"No doubt. How is she?"

"Still about the same. Her bruises look better, but there hasn't been any change to her condition. The doctor said that the internal swelling has gone down a lot."

"Well at least that's good to hear." Adrian looked concerned. "What do you guys normally do when she's in town?"

Chelsea smiled, though her eyes were glassy with tears. "Oh, having Joss around is the best. We like to go to the beach, of course, and we hang out with my daughter, so we do a lot of kid-friendly things. S'mores and movies. Games and puzzles. But when Karsyn goes to bed, we have a glass of wine and laugh about the past." She suddenly touched her hand to her lips in disbelief. *I remembered that.*

"Sounds like a lot of the stuff I do with my brothers' and sister's families," Adrian chuckled.

"Are you guys close?"

"You know, we're closer now than when we were little. They are all a lot older than me, so I get to spoil their kids. It's nice. Plus, we get to pass down all the stuff we used to do growing up around here."

"You grew up here?" Chelsea panicked. She didn't remember if they went to school together …

"Not exactly *here* here. About an hour north, along the mainland coast. A little town called 'Attaway.'"

"Oh OK." She had no idea where that was.

"What about you?"

"I ..." Chelsea panicked. She couldn't remember the name her street. *You got this.* "Not far from here. We had a little house in central Sorel Island and hit the different beaches here all the time growing up. It just feels like home."

"I've never been anywhere like it," Adrian said. His gaze grew intense as he looked deep into her eyes.

Blushing, Chelsea glanced away and saw Samantha staring at her with raised eyebrows. "So, does your family still live close?"

"Yeah. My sister is still in Attaway with her family, and one of my brothers is in Hampton." Adrian glanced at his watch. "You know, I was wondering—"

"Adrian!" Cassidy had just emerged from the kitchen with a to-go bag and set it on the counter in front of him.

"Ah, that's my cue." He accidentally brushed Chelsea's hand as he scooped up the bag.

Chelsea shivered. "Well, it was nice talking to you." Hurriedly, she scrambled back into the kitchen and leaned against the counter. *What am I sixteen?*

Not missing her chance, Samantha whirled into the kitchen behind her, crossed her arms, and gave her a knowing smile. She tapped her chin with her finger a moment and then shrugged and walked away.

"Good grief, Samantha," Chelsea muttered. But she couldn't help but wonder if everyone else knew how hard her heart was pounding.

Chapter Twelve

Chelsea felt like her entire body was fizzing like a freshly poured soda. She shivered and let a smile play about her lips as she recalled the sensation of talking to Adrian. It was something that felt completely and utterly breathless for her. That's when she realized that she had been holding her breath since she escaped to the kitchen.

Breathing in deeply, Chelsea pulled herself out of the feeling of elation that was coursing through her. Immediately, she turned her thoughts to Julian and the fact that she's supposed to be in a relationship with him. The thought was instantly sobering.

I was apparently carrying his baby! I at least need to give this guy a chance. She wasn't excited though. It wasn't like when she saw Adrian.

Weighed down by guilt, Chelsea pulled her phone out. She hesitated. *Maybe. Maybe not. Ugh. I should.* She opened it and began texting.

Hi! I know it's been a few days. Did you want to grab dinner on Wednesday?

Her hand hovered over the send button. Was she thinking clearly? Should she wait awhile and then try? Was it OK to be totally impulsive about the feeling of duty that was now surging through her, overcoming the joy like a tidal wave?

But aren't we here, on this planet, to seek joy? It's the twenty-first century! What allegiance do I owe him? We aren't married! If a relationship is based on feelings and I have none, then why pursue it …

Chelsea set her phone on the counter and put her head in her hands. What a mess.

A tray of cheesecake tarts topped with strawberry jam were conveniently close. She snagged one and turned around, leaning on the counter again as she savored each bite.

Breathe. I don't have to make a decision today. My memory may come back later this week, and I can decide then. But until I decide …

Chelsea's phone buzzed on the counter.

Julian: "Hey, how are you doing today?"

OK, maybe that was a sign …

She stared at the message preview a couple minutes and then opened the phone. She deleted her previous message.

Chelsea: "I'm good. How are you?"
Julian: "Good. Busy day at the office."
Chelsea: "Ah, well that's good."
Julian: "I was wondering if you're free tomorrow evening. Maybe we could grab dinner."

A long pause ... *clearly, that's a sign* ... and then Chelsea set her jaw and started typing.

Chelsea: "Sure, that would be nice."

If I want to get my life back on track, this might help. At least this is something that I would normally be doing, right? And normal is healthy, and that should trigger my memories ... I hope.

* * *

Washed Up was a small bar food restaurant with a wrap-around covered porch right on the water, facing the mainland. There was a cool little bar attached where the sea breeze played with the fringe along the awning and boats could drive up and order food to go.

Chelsea sipped her lemon water and gazed across the bay. The mainland was barely visible, and she wondered if somewhere other people were struggling to recall their lives the same way she was. Or if some of them were trying to escape. It didn't make much sense for her to run away to the mainland. Most people would choose to run away to the island. She was already supposed to be in paradise—

"Chelsea?"

Blinking, Chelsea turned back to her dining partner. Julian was gazing questioningly at her.

"You OK?"

"Yeah, yeah, I'm fine. Just, uh—" she let out a sigh, "enjoying being on the water. It's been a trying day … actually every day since the accident has been trying."

Julian shifted uncomfortably. "I know. I can't imagine what you're going through right now." He took a sip from his soda. "Did you get to see Jocelyn today?"

"I did. I went first thing this morning. She's looking better every day but still not moving."

"I see." He reached across the table and placed his hand on hers. Then he gazed into her eyes, which gave Chelsea the sense that he really did care and was trying to be there for her.

She forced a smile. "I really appreciate your patience and support. I'm sure this is tough for you too."

"I know you need time to recover. I love you, and I'm not going anywhere."

Unconsciously, Chelsea flinched and tightened her lips. "I'm glad."

Julian suddenly looked like he didn't believe her. He pulled his hand back and looked out across the water himself.

The guilt rising again, Chelsea decided it was time to share what she knew. "I saw my therapist the other day. I don't know if you knew I had seen one after the divorce."

Julian looked back at Chelsea, crossed his arms, and leaned on the table. "Annie. Yeah. You've seen her this spring too."

So he wasn't going to say it. But she couldn't blame him. He probably didn't want to bring up anything that could upset her. "She told me that I had a miscarriage and saw her after that." Chelsea briefed him on the conversation. "I don't remember it at all. I can't even think of what it was like to be pregnant, not even with Karsyn."

Julian was quiet.

After a couple minutes, Chelsea started to get pissed. "Aren't you even going to say anything?"

"Chelse, I don't know what to say." He spoke firmly, but not without love. "We were both excited about the baby when we found out, and then that happened just a couple weeks later. We worked through it together. It was hard. This whole spring has been hard. We've had a lot of challenges."

"*We*? *We*'ve had challenges?" Chelsea choked back her feelings for a moment, not fully understanding them. "I'm confused. I keep finding out things that I supposedly did, things that happened to *my body*, and I don't even remember them. It's like I'm in this foreign *thing*." She shook her hands, gesturing at her chest. "It's not fully mine. It belonged to before-the-accident Chelsea." Then she gasped and her eyes grew wide. "What if my soul left and another one entered my body and that's why I don't remember this stuff." She realized that she was starting to sound crazy but honestly didn't care.

"Chelse, hey, it's OK—"

"But it's NOT OK! It's not OK at all. How can this be happening? And I thought Annie could help me, and I just ended up more confused."

Julian scooted his chair around till he was beside her at the two-person table. He put his hand on her shoulder, and she looked at him nervously. "You're right. It's not OK. But, I'm not sure what I can do other than just sit with you through this. I'll talk to you about anything you want to know. Maybe it will help you remember—"

"Now I'm wondering if I even *want* to remember everything. Maybe that accident happened *for me*. Maybe it was supposed to protect me by giving me a clean slate and letting me move on with my life."

Chelsea didn't know why she felt like lashing out at Julian, but she did. He was an easy target, just taking it like he was. And he was so unruffled that it pissed her off even more.

"Alright, look, you're getting prickly now. I don't think you're being fair to yourself or me or our memories together."

Chelsea burst into tears.

Julian wrapped his arms around her and just held her for a moment. "I understand. It's OK to cry."

But somehow, Chelsea didn't feel like it was. It never was. This wasn't normal for her. She's not a crier. She's a feelings stuffer. She's a go-get-a-cocktail-and-don't-feel-anything person.

When did she become a feeler?

A voice whispered in her ear, "*Lean in.*"

Chelsea gasped and sat up. She grabbed a napkin, wiped her tears, and blew her nose as softly as she could. "I'm sorry. You didn't deserve that. I'm a mess right now."

Julian let go and sat back. "I understand. Really."

"It's just incredibly scary not knowing what came before the past few days." Chelsea cleared her throat. She could hear "Lean in" echoing in her head and hoped it was Zara. She also hoped the message was for her to lean into the feelings and not to lean into the strange relationship she found herself in.

"And I don't expect you to jump right back in where we left off. Like I said before, I want to spend time with you and give you time to recover your memories. I'm patient. And I love you. I'm not going anywhere."

"What was next? For our future?" Chelsea peered at him expectantly.

"You wanted me to meet Jocelyn, of course. And Karsyn."

"Like how soon?"

Julian smiled weakly. "I was going to meet them both at your birthday party."

"That's pretty soon ..." Chelsea sipped her water and sighed.

"It is. But we can wait. There's no reason to rush."

Chelsea half smiled. "Thank you." Then her smile faded as she recalled that pinpoint memory of the boy who made her feel so uncomfortable. "You know, I have a tiny bit of memory from a boyfriend I had a long time ago. His name was ... Vic. It's Vic. We dated toward the end of high school. He used to tell me terrible things about myself and make me feel ridiculous. He would trip me in the halls and then laugh as he kept me from falling. He talked about how all my friends were worthless and didn't really like me for who I was."

"That's awful. I hope you didn't date him long."

"Just a few months. But it really destroyed me. I don't think I dated anyone for a long time after that. And I'm not sure why I have such strong memories of that relationship that they are the first ones coming up. Not us."

"I don't know either, especially since I don't remember you mentioning this before. I realize that we don't know all the details of each other's history, but this clearly had a big impact on you. I'm surprised it hasn't come up."

Frowning, Chelsea leaned back and gazed at the sea a moment. "Me too. But maybe this is why I'm struggling so much to remember us. Maybe I need to heal something from my past first."

Reaching across the table, Julian put his hand on hers. "I don't want to give you any more trauma, so maybe we should keep taking things slow for a while. I want to move forward too, but not if it's stressful or hard for you."

Just then, their entrees arrived. When the server left their table, Chelsea smiled, for real this time. "Thanks for understanding. I think what we are doing now is fine. Let's take it slow, and hopefully my memory of us will return."

When Chelsea got back to her house, she realized two things—she didn't feel any sparks with Julian, but she did feel like a jerk.

Chapter Thirteen

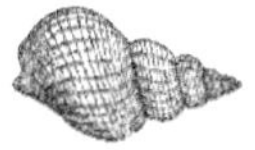

The next morning, as Karsyn got on the bus, Chelsea felt the sea calling to her. Instead of getting right in her car, she answered with open arms.

As she crossed the street, the salt in the air tickled her nostrils, encouraging her to let out a huge breath. She noticed that she had been holding her breath a lot lately, waiting for the rest of the story to come. Knowing that she would eventually have to make a choice about Julian wasn't easy. Neither was waiting for her sister to wake up. Also, falling back into the routine of motherhood, which still felt unnatural. Actually, nearly everything felt weird, and her trepidations nearly overtook her several times a day. But Chelsea knew she had to push forward, if for no other reason than the little sweetie that she put on the bus every morning who was her sun and moon and stars. And all the realms of the Universe.

Plus, she had to remember.

Sitting down in the sand, Chelsea watched the sea massaging the beach, coaxing it to come play. She closed her eyes and listened to the waves crashing, just like when she was little. It was strange that something so simple continued on, day after day, century after century as cities rose and fell, as people lived and died, as the earth turned and changed. And here she was, a speck on the beach, staring out across the cerulean endlessness, wondering about life.

What made the Universe choose to keep her intact while her sister lay motionless in the hospital. *Am I supposed to learn a lesson? What did I ask for? How am I supposed to keep going if she doesn't make it?*

Breathe in. Breathe out. Breathe in. Breathe out. She slowed her breathing to pattern with the waves and felt like one with the earth. The sun glinted off the water the color of sea glass.

She stayed a moment more, till she felt peace wash over her from head to toe. The longer she spent staring at the ocean, the more she felt grounded, like the desire to run had almost completely passed. It seemed to have been pushed to a tiny corner of her mind, and it barely peeked above the surface to disturb her now. Her roots were stronger. She was settling in. Happily.

"I can keep going," she whispered. Then she rose, brushed the sand from her denim clam diggers, and meandered back to her car.

Driving straight to the hospital, Chelsea seemed overly aware of the life around her. It felt like she was walking in a bubble while the rest of the world bustled on around her. She had to shake the foreboding feeling before she got to Jocelyn's hospital room. Hospitals are sad enough without bringing it in with you.

As she entered the hospital, the golden sun flooded through the entryway, glistening on the freshly shined floor. *Maybe this will be OK. Maybe I just need to carry the sunshine with me today.* Approaching the room felt like slow motion. *Why am I so aware of every second today? It's like time is slowing down.*

She paused at the doorway and looked in. Everything seemed the same. It was always the same in Jocelyn's room.

"Hey sis." She sat in the chair beside her bed. "It's Chelsea." Taking her hand, Chelsea stroked the back of it, feeling the warmth.

"Jocelyn, things are so weird without you. I need you to get better." Chelsea paused. "It feels weird to say your name. I guess it's been a while since you've responded to it. It's like I'm always talking *about* you, not really *to* you."

Her phone buzzed, and she glanced at it. Megan had texted, just checking on her. She could answer later.

Gazing at her sister, Chelsea took in the perfection of her face. The cuts were nearly healed, the bruises faded drastically. Yet ... she was still here. She looked like she was just sleeping.

"Where are you? What are you thinking about?" Chelsea said. "Can you hear me?" she whispered.

Jocelyn's chest rose and fell, but there was no other movement.

Watching Jocelyn, suddenly Chelsea felt hot and started shaking. *This doesn't seem real.* She felt like she wasn't in her own body. *I need to ground myself before I freak out.*

Still holding Jocelyn's hand, Chelsea closed her eyes. She listened to the heart monitor and slowed her breathing to match it. She began a meditation in her mind as she sat quietly. A chill ran over her from toes to cheeks.

"The Universe sees you and hears you. You have no need to be afraid. You asked for a great change. You didn't know you were asking, but it has been playing in your mind a long time. You are in the middle of this change. This is why you feel so upside-down."

"I didn't ask for anyone to get hurt," Chelsea whispered.

"Fear not. Great things are coming. Large and small."

"Zara, that doesn't make any sense," Chelsea whispered. She knew it was Zara's voice relaying a message from beyond, but she couldn't see her. She seemed to only have one sense or the other when it came to Zara's presence. Never a full picture.

"Sometimes the Universe has to shake things up to get you to correct your course."

The voice melted away, and suddenly, in Chelsea's mind's eye, she could see an elephant only a breath away from her. It gazed softly into her eyes.

For a minute, Chelsea reveled in its beauty. It had a purple tint, like the sun was setting as it shown on the creature. She could feel the depth of wisdom it held within.

Slowly, she tried reaching out in her mind's eye to touch the elephant's trunk. A powerful flood of love coursed into her body. At first, she felt herself bristle at the surge, but then, she forced herself to let her walls down. *It's safe. Zara sent her.* Chelsea channeled the feeling through herself and felt the warmth. It was like being wrapped in a blanket fresh from the drier while sipping tea, a full inside and out feeling of safety and love.

I need to share this. She pictured the love from the elephant surrounding her sister too, and soon, in her mind's eye, a huge minty green bubble of love and warmth enveloped them. It was green like sea glass. Like home.

In that moment, a memory broke through.

"I found another one," she called. Her parents were laughing about some private joke. Her mother carried a red bucket. Chelsea ran over and placed something in it.

Jocelyn raced over to peek in. "That's five!"

"That's a lot for this trip," their dad said.

The girls were probably five, Karsyn's age. Chelsea stepped back and took in the scene from her past. Her dad was wearing a white t-shirt with an elephant on it streaked with rainbow. *I remember that shirt!*

"Here's another," their mom said. Both girls raced over, and their mom knelt in the sand, something precious in her hand.

Chelsea gazed at the sea glass, a newer piece that hadn't been fully smoothed by the surf. It wasn't jagged, but it looked like pieces had been pulled out like taffy from the center. It was strange and twisted and beautiful. Her mother plunked it into the bucket. Chelsea couldn't resist throwing her arms around her. Jocelyn followed suit.

Her mom laughed as she almost fell over, and their dad put a hand on her back to keep her upright. Chelsea felt the green bubble that she sat in intensify ten-fold.

The scene started to fade. *I miss you guys.* A tear trickled down her cheek in real life. *I need strength to get through all this.*

Beep.

Chelsea's eyes popped open. That beep was off cadence. Was her heart rate speeding up? She looked at Jocelyn in the bed. No change. But that beep was a little faster.

Just then, a nurse peeked in, "Everything OK?" She immediately approached Jocelyn, looked at something on a tablet in her hand, and then took some vital signs.

Chelsea sat quietly for a moment, but she had to ask. "Is her heart rate higher?"

"Just a little. It's been a very low resting rate since she came in, but it seems to have increased a couple beats a minute now. Maybe she senses that you're here."

Chelsea smiled. "Thanks. I needed to hear that."

"It's a good sign." The nurse smiled too.

***

That evening, Chelsea decided to return to the beach to walk. She threw on a long-sleeve boat-neck top and walking shorts (running shorts? Did she like running? Who knows?) Her pensive mood hadn't changed, especially since Zara had visited at the hospital. She felt more at peace with Jocelyn's situation, though. The nurse had said the slight increase in heart rate was a good sign, and Chelsea was ready to embrace that.

Come back to us Joss!

Feeling a little lighter than she did that morning, Chelsea crossed the street and slipped off her sandals. Just sinking her feet into the sand felt like therapy. It was always there for her. She continued south, the sun settling over the island to her right.

Breathing in deeply, she let the salt air sooth her soul. Children dug in the sand and built sandcastles with their families, wrapped in sweatshirts as the air chilled. Couples walked by, laughing and talking. It was truly a perfect evening.

Chelsea focused on where she was and everything she could sense around her. She smelled and tasted the salt in the air. She felt the breeze on her legs, the sand on her feet. The sound of waves accompanied her joyfully as she strolled. And the sights, so many! Late spring on a beach in New England was always glorious in her eyes. It felt like a million years since she had enjoyed an evening walk on the beach in such perfect weather.

Her heart was happy.

She stopped walking and gazed out at the ocean in all its perfection. Crossing her arms, she tipped her head back and closed her eyes. Peace.

"Enjoying the evening?" a familiar voice spoke a few feet away, and it made her arms and legs tingle.

Chelsea opened her eyes and looked at the speaker. "Oh," she stammered, taking him all in.

Adrian must have been running. His face glistened with sweat, and his t-shirt was wet in the middle of his chest. For the first time, she noticed how built he was and observed how his shirt clung to his muscular arms and chest. Quite different from the suit he usually wore.

Then she smiled. "Hey, yes, it's so nice out. I had to get a walk in and enjoy it."

"Me too. Perfect night for a run. Couldn't resist."

"Yeah, I was just absorbing all this gorgeousness." She gestured toward the ocean. "Trying to clear my head. The last few days have been ... busy." Chelsea looked back at the sea.

"Same here." Adrian followed her gaze for a moment before looking back at her. "I know it's not my business, but are you OK? You look ... pained."

Chelsea looked back at him and realized that she was carrying her truth on her forehead. The tightness finally noticed, she massaged her forehead a little and looked back at him, unsure of what to say. "I'm fine. It's just ... a lot. A lot has happened. And it's confusing. And I'm worried. That's all."

"No need to explain unless you feel like it. I was just concerned. You don't usually look so pensive when I see you at work."

"Well, it's hard to be sad in a bakery," Chelsea laughed.

"True. But it's hard to be sad at the beach too." Adrian cocked his head and watched her for a moment. "Is this usually where you go to think?"

She paused before answering and then looked at his amber-brown eyes. "You'll think this is weird, but I'm actually not sure."

"It's OK. We all have something going on. Do you know what makes me feel better, though?"

Chelsea gave him a half smile. "What's that?"

"There's a place nearby that I like to visit. It always takes my breath away. It's special. Want to go see it?"

"You're not going to tell me what it is?"

"Nope. It's a surprise. I'm parked over there. Want to go?"

"Why not?" Chelsea followed Adrian back to a black Jeep with the top off. "This is your ride?"

"Yeah, you wouldn't expect a guy in finance to drive this, I know, but I've had this car for years. It's fun, and it gets me everywhere I need to go."

"Not judging. I'm actually looking forward to riding with my hair whipping in the wind," she laughed.

They both climbed in, and Adrian drove them about ten minutes to the southernmost point on the island.

Chelsea gasped when they pulled up. Trees crowded around the edge of the lot and stretched on in either direction with just a small break where she could glimpse the endless sea to the south. The sand almost sparkled with the sheer volume of shells and things that had washed up. It was a treasure trove of deep-sea flotsam. She glanced at the sign tucked in among the trees. "Bottle Beach? This is where you go?"

"Yeah, have you been here?"

"I ... yes, I think so. It's really familiar. I think ... it was a long time ago. Give me a minute, maybe it will come back."

Adrian gave her a sideways glance and raised his eyebrows as he hopped out of the car. "Want to walk with me here?"

"I do." Chelsea nodded and grinned. There was something about this place that called her.

When they both walked out to the beach, Chelsea could see the sand shimmer in the late evening sun. They started walking down the beach.

"A lot of shells wash up here, along with sea glass and chunks of broken bottles. It's because of the way the Gulf Stream flows. It's like it just drops everything off right here. I've always loved this beach. It's unique. Not great for walking barefoot in the water necessarily. But it's neat to just sit and look at all the pieces. I always feel like it's a metaphor for life. You go through some serious shit, and then you wash up here at the end of your journey. Then you get to see the sun and the sky again."

"I know what you mean ... I've always found sea glass interesting for that reason. My sister and I used to collect it when we were little. I always felt like I was rescuing it and giving it a new life by taking it home with me. We had a huge jar that I still have at my house. I got to keep it by default because Joss left to traipse around the world."

"That's nice. I'm glad someone could give it a home."

"I'm glad it was me." But something didn't feel right about that. What was the strange feeling rising in her stomach? She brushed it away. "I think I have been here before." A memory flooded through her, and she suddenly stopped. She gasped. "We used to come here all the time when we were little. Oh! This is where we got the sea glass. This is what I remembered this morning. My parents took us here. And the red bucket full of sea glass." She talked fast as the pieces all connected.

"That's good. I'm glad you remembered that," Adrian looked at her and furrowed his brow.

Chelsea returned his look. "You must think I'm pretty strange right now."

"Not really. We all forget things, especially from our childhood. You can't store everything in your brain. Gotta make room for new memories, right?"

"Well, that's not the whole truth of it." Chelsea looked back at the sea. "I know we just met recently, so I feel weird sharing this, but I'm having trouble remembering anything from before the wreck. Even important details. It's been strange."

Adrian put his hands in his pockets. "It makes sense. Whether you hit your head, or your body just decided to protect you for a while, I don't think it's that odd that you lost your memory." He looked back at her and smiled. "And we didn't just meet. I've been coming in The Salty Cupcake for a couple years. It's close to my work."

"Oh? Well, you see, I didn't remember," Chelsea chuckled self-consciously.

"Maybe it's a good thing. We get to start afresh." Adrian touched her arm. "Besides, I don't think you even gave me a second look till after the accident, so it can't all be bad."

Chelsea looked back at Adrian and felt herself melting as she gazed into his eyes. The faintest scent of his cologne wafted on the salty breeze tantalizingly. "No, I guess it's not all bad." She smiled, blushed, and then looked back at the ocean as the waves continued their never-ending romance with the shore.

Chapter Fourteen

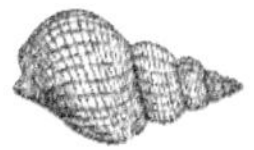

The next day, Chelsea awoke feeling giddy. She did a little dance as she got dressed and then focused on the needs for the day: The Salty Cupcake, Joss, and Karsyn.

She had an end-of-year brunch with Karsyn that morning, as she finished kindergarten, and The Salty Cupcake was a sponsor. A quick trip to the bakery, and she loaded her car with bagels, scones, and doughnuts.

After the brunch, she gave Karsyn a big hug and promised to see her on Sunday night. She was spending the weekend with Damon, who was also at the brunch. Both parents had beamed as Karsyn dragged them to meet her friends and piled her plate with treats. It was a fun event, but Chelsea knew she would miss her daughter over the weekend.

After the brunch, she went back to the hospital to see Jocelyn. Her heart rate was still in the normal resting range since the strange incident with Zara and the elephant. Chelsea was relieved that she at least had that improvement under her belt. It was a start.

Back at her townhouse, she wasn't sure how to kill time till she was supposed to meet Samantha at six thirty p.m. at the bakery to do inventory for her farmer's market run in the morning.

What did I do before when I was alone? Did I have a hobby? Did I like movies? Maybe a movie.

Chelsea collapsed on the couch in the living room. Flicking on Netflix, she scrolled through genres, but nothing was appealing. In fact, nothing looked familiar. *Pretty weird that I remember how to use the TV, but I can't remember my own life ...*

Then she looked through the DVR and finally found a series that sounded interesting. It was ... vaguely. She watched a couple episodes and played a game on her phone till it was time to grab dinner and head to the bakery.

As she drove, she couldn't help but think that she had somehow calmed over the past few days. Right after the accident, quiet and "nothing to do" made her feel antsy. She wanted to run. But now ... maybe she was just getting back into her routine. "Maybe rest is OK?" she said out loud.

She pulled into her usual spot but entered through the front door. Looking around, she did a minor assessment. Everything looked pretty new, which made sense since she just did a remodel. No scuffed paint or beat up corners. The glass case was clean. For the first time, though, she really looked at what she had built.

In just a few years, she had created her dream. She ran a bakery. A successful bakery! That's not something easy to do. Not everyone can do this. A smile spread across her face.

I'm really proud of this. It's amazing! Grandma would be so proud of me! She smiled and felt warmth envelop her heart.

"Hey Chelse. Let's start with the case and then move to the kitchen," Samantha said as she burst through the kitchen door.

"Sounds good," Chelsea said. She approached the counter case full of treats and read through the labels. She mentioned a couple they were low on, and Samantha compared with the master list, adding the next week's goods to a separate sheet.

Together, they went into the kitchen and sorted through cupboards and the walk-in fridge and freezer.

"If Tamsyn's Jams is there tomorrow, get three large jars of her strawberry champagne jam. That will be perfect for the jelly-filled doughnuts for next week."

"Have we used that before?"

"We use it every spring when we do those doughnuts," Samantha said. "Still no memory of this stuff?"

"Not really. I don't think much has come back except a couple childhood memories." Color rose in her cheeks as she recalled her conversation with Adrian at Bottle Beach.

"Huh," Samantha said. "Anything you'd like to share? Did you get hot all of a sudden?"

"You don't miss anything do you?" Chelsea said. She briefed Samantha on running into Adrian.

"I'm enjoying this saga. Let me know when the next episode is on. I want to tune in," she laughed.

Chelsea pushed back through the door to the restaurant. "Of course! What's left to do here? Let me help you finish up for the day."

"Actually, Jada just swept up and left. Kelli restocked. I think we are pretty good unless you wanted to grab a couple things out of the case to take home."

Chelsea eyed up the mini-cinni rolls. "Yeah, I should grab a couple of those before they get too stale to sell."

"I'll get you a box. Do you want to flip off the 'Open' sign?"

"Got it!" Chelsea strode to the front of the store where the switch was beside the window. The sky was turning pink from the sunset. Even though the building across the street partially blocked her view, she could still see the gorgeous colors filtering up through the sky. She watched a cloud for a moment and then noticed someone running down the street. As she flicked the switch, their eyes met. He grinned and waved, slowing to a stop in front of the window.

Two nights in a row? Maybe my luck is changing. Chelsea pushed the door open and leaned in the doorway. "Hi!"

"Hey! Another gorgeous night for a run! What are you doing here?"

"Checking inventory for my farmer's market run tomorrow. I just wrapped up my list and was ready to close."

"Nice! What are you up to the rest of the evening?"

"I was about to grab some of the mini-cinni rolls and head home. I honestly don't know what I used to do before the accident in my spare time, so I'm exploring right now. I might dig through my closet and see if I had a hobby or paint my toenails or something."

Adrian shook his head. "Wow, a clean slate. You know, you don't have to go back to what you used to do. You can do whatever you want."

"That's true ... I can start a new hobby." She stepped back from the door. "Did you want to come in while we're talking?"

"Sure." Adrian followed her inside. "If I picked a new hobby, it would be baking, but you clearly already have that one checked off."

"Clearly," Chelsea laughed. Just then, Samantha came back from the kitchen.

"I grabbed a box for you, but Brent called. He needs me to grab milk on the way home—hi! I didn't realize anyone else was here."

"I can go. I was just talking—"

"No, no, hon. She's the boss anyway. I was just about to leave ... unless Chelsea needs me for anything else?" Samantha smiled with her lips closed and opened her eyes wide at Chelsea.

Chelsea flared her nostrils and gazed back at Samantha trying not to laugh. "I'm good. You can head out."

"Have a great night!" Samantha called as she grabbed her purse and dashed out the door.

After Samantha left, Adrian turned back to Chelsea who was pulling her treats out of the case for the weekend. The smell was heavenly.

"So what hobby do you think you'll try first? Maybe golf? Parasailing? No wait. Base-jumping. You look like a base-jumper." His broad grin made her heart do flip flops.

Chelsea laughed. "You got me. Actually, I was thinking something a little calmer. Maybe I'll try to knit or write a romance novel. My sister has a blog, so maybe the writing thing would be my thing too."

"I can't see you knitting. No offense."

"Not sure that's really attractive to me anyway. Pretty sure I would get halfway through and just have a tangled pile of yarn."

"So, what about the novel? Do you think you've ever tried to write before?"

Chelsea stared at the wall a moment and encouraged a memory to surface. Nothing truly did though. "I'm not sure. I feel like I would enjoy it. I feel like I've done something with writing before. No idea if it was just for English classes or a longer project. I can't get a feel for it."

"That would be a fun thing to try. I've never been a big creative. I took a ballroom dancing class once. And I tried to make a mosaic with my niece. It looked like a kid made it, so I let her take the credit." They both laughed.

"Ballroom dancing, huh? I'd like to see that."

"I was pretty good at it. Here." He pulled out his phone and turned on a song.

"You keep classical music on your phone?"

"I listen to it sometimes when I run. I know that seems weird, but it's really good for me to decompress, especially in the evening. I don't want to get all pumped up and then want to tear through a wall when I really need to get to sleep."

"Good point. So, show me some moves."

Adrian motioned for Chelsea to step forward and took her in his arms. A flutter in her chest nearly made Chelsea giggle, but she maintained her composure and just smiled.

As the music played, Adrian guided Chelsea in a waltz around the bakery. While she danced, Chelsea felt his strong hand on her back and the gentle way he twirled her around. He really was a good dancer, and the smoothness of their dance put Chelsea at ease more than she had been in days.

As Adrian relaxed into his lead role and his moves all came back to him, his face softened from a look of concentration to pride. He clearly liked what he was doing, and he had a command of the floor that Chelsea loved.

As the music swelled, Adrian pulled Chelsea closer, and she could smell the same note of his cologne as the night before at the beach. He was warm but not sweaty, thankfully, and Chelsea gently leaned into him as he led her around the room again.

Another twirl at the end of the song, and Adrian brought Chelsea back close. She was still on her toes from turning, and her face was inches from his. She could feel the warmth from his breath, and the tightness of his arms around her. As their eyes locked, Chelsea gazed deeply into his beautiful amber-brown eyes, and he seemed lost in her sea green ones.

Gently, he let go of her hand and tipped her chin toward him. Then he kissed her like he had waited years for the moment. And Chelsea returned the kiss hungrily.

When Chelsea realized what she was doing though, she gently pulled back, breathing hard, with her heart pounding dangerously against her rib cage. It felt like magic holding her there, but then that twinge of guilt wrapped itself around her like vines. She didn't truly have a blank slate.

"I'm sorry. I shouldn't have done that," Adrian said. "I was caught up in the moment."

Breathless, Chelsea whispered, "Me too."

Adrian ran a hand through his hair. "I'll walk you to your car," he offered.

Chelsea blinked, still breathless and not sure whether she should be pissed or elated. "Sure, thank you ... Do you want a cookie?"

"Sorry?" Adrian too was regaining his composure. He took a deep breath and looked at her.

Chelsea laughed at her own embarrassment. "I asked if you wanted a cookie."

"A cookie? Was it that good?" Adrian grinned.

"The dancing was." Chelsea winked.

"Huh." Adrian put his hands on his hips and looked at Chelsea like she had challenged him. "Yeah, I'll take that cookie. I earned it."

Chelsea chuckled as she selected a big chocolate chunk cookie from the case and smiled deviously as she handed it to him. He took a bite and gave her a thumbs up.

Adrian walked her to her car and continued down the street, finishing his cookie before resuming his run. Chelsea sat in the car a moment and just watched him. "What am I doing? I'm supposed to be dating Julian. What am I supposed to do?"

When she got home, Chelsea parked and went straight to the beach to walk and clear her head in the twilight. The thoughts shooting through her brain were like a meteor shower, vivid and fast and abundant.

"OK, Universe," she muttered, "what am I supposed to do? Give me a sign."

A rumble of thunder rippled across the sky. A butterfly passed right in front of her.

"Got it. Time to head home."

Chapter Fifteen

"Where are the butterflies?" Chelsea whispered. Her voice sounded heavy.

"I didn't send any. This was for your greatest and highest good."

"How is this good?"

"It's in your soul contract. Your soul decided on certain things before you were born that would happen in this lifetime so your soul could learn and grow."

Pause. Then Chelsea said, "My soul must be totally insane to agree to this stuff."

"You're growing."

"What if I want to stay the same?"

"That's not why you're here."

Pause. "So why am I here?" Chelsea sounded a little snarky.

"To grow. To become who you truly are."

"I love you, but sometimes I hate you."

Zara laughed. "I know. I love you always."

Chelsea realized that she was dreaming as she watched her sister come into focus and try to put on a pair of boots. They were clearly too small, but she kept jamming her foot in. Finally, she threw them down.

She walked in a circle around the boots and then tried again.

"Zara …" Chelsea whispered. Zara didn't respond. She just kept trying to put the boots on. As Chelsea watched, Zara repeated the pattern several more times. Finally, a harp started playing in the distance. Time to get up.

Chelsea opened her eyes and rolled onto her side, the wisps of the dream wafting away. "What was Zara trying to tell me?" She closed her eyes again and pictured Zara pulling the boots on, looking frustrated, and then pulling them off again. "Something doesn't fit … do I own boots? What do boots mean to me? Nothing I can think of."

She rolled onto her back and stared at the ceiling. "No idea if I even have boots …" Sighing, she shifted her gaze to the window where she could see the sun rising. Her thoughts lightened, and the warm memory of kissing Adrian washed over her. A tingle spread from her face to her chest and gave her goosebumps on her arms as she remembered the tender but longing way he had kissed her.

Letting out a long breath, Chelsea placed her hands over her heart and replayed the scene from the night before. Chatting with Adrian … then dancing … the way she felt so light and airy when he led her around the restaurant and gazed into her eyes. She let her mind wander back to that kiss and held it there, feeling his energy around her. Clearly, he was as attracted as she was. There was only one problem …

A tiny twinge of guilt ruined the memory, and she sat up in bed with a sour look on her face. She recoiled from the thought of Julian. Yes, he's nice, but there just aren't any feelings there. Yet? Or was there before the accident? "Hey Universe, *what* am I supposed to do? How can I make this easy?" Immediately, her mind flashed back to Zara trying on the boots. "You could be clearer ..." she muttered.

After a quick shower, Chelsea drank a protein shake and threw her purse in her flamingo tote. She gathered the reusable totes for the farmers market and started down the stairs when she paused. "Huh." She jogged the rest of the way down the stairs and flung open the coat closet. "No rain boots. No tall boots. One pair of booties." Chelsea picked up the booties and examined the soles, which looked like they had seen better days. "Do I wear these?" She made a mental note to buy new booties for fall. "I guess the boots Zara had weren't mine. So, who did they belong to?"

Pulling out her phone, she texted Samantha.

"Am I crazy?"

After a moment with no response, she put the phone back in her bag.

Almost immediately, her phone buzzed, and she looked at the screen. Damon. "Hey, everything OK?" she answered.

"Hi Mommy!"

"Hey Cupcake, how's your morning?"

"I miss you. Daddy said I could call to see if I can go to the farmer's market with you."

"Oh," Chelsea paused. "Sure, I can pick you up now if you're ready. Can I talk to Daddy a minute?"

"Daddy, it's Mommy," Karsyn whispered loudly.

"Hi, Chelse. She was really missing you last night, and I just thought of it this morning. I know you always go on Saturday."

Chelsea laughed. "It's fine. I just wanted to make sure that you knew she called and asked."

"Yeah, I can see why you would wonder. What time should I have her ready?"

"I was about to leave now. Will she be ready in a few minutes?"

"Yeah, she's already had breakfast. I'll get her dressed."

"Sounds good."

"Hey Chelse, do you want to spend the weekend with her? It's OK to say 'no.' I'm here all weekend. I just thought you might want a little extra time right now, since you can take it easy. I'm assuming you canceled your birthday party since Joss is in the hospital."

Ugh, the birthday party. Am I supposed to cancel that? Who was invited? "Spending time with Karsyn would be nice. Thanks for being so understanding."

"Not a problem."

When Chelsea hung up, she knew it would be nice to spend a little time with Karsyn. In fact, she was excited. Now she would have a distraction to keep her from floating back to the moment she kissed Adrian and wondering what she was supposed to do about Julian.

Plus, she needed some mommy-daughter time.

At Damon's townhouse, Karsyn was sitting on the front porch with her pink sequined messenger bag across her shoulder. She waved and jumped up and down, lights flashing from her tennis shoes, when Chelsea pulled in the drive. Damon approached the car with Karsyn's car seat, and the pair was on their way in just a few minutes.

As she drove, a text came through, and she peeked at a stoplight. It was from Samantha.

"It's normal to feel weird. You were in a bad car wreck! Yes, you're crazy, but really, who isn't?"

Chelsea smiled. At least this was "normal." Things had to fall back into place after everything is up in the air, right? Shouldn't all the pieces come back to land?

When she parked, Chelsea answered.

"True. Hey, was my birthday party supposed to be today?"

A moment later, Samantha answered.

"I texted our friends and told them it's postponed. Don't worry. Glad I had the guest list."

"Thanks. Really glad you're on top of things."

At the farmer's market, Karsyn pulled Chelsea to the craft tents first. *How does anyone bring a kid here and not drop a fortune?* Karsyn wanted *everything—*

hair clips, an apron, another purse, a painting of a mermaid hugging a narwhal. "OK, I'll get that. We can hang it above your bed. It matches your bedroom colors," Chelsea reasoned. She felt completely blindsided by Karsyn's love of shopping. *Has she always been like this?*

"We need to pick up stuff for the shop before everything closes, Karse," Chelsea said.

"Can we get strawberries for home?" Karsyn said, not missing a beat.

Want, want, want ... "Yeah, we can. Let's make sure we get all the store stuff first, though." Chelsea shifted the painting to her other arm and followed Karsyn through the crowd to the fruit stand wondering how she would carry it all.

"Oh, Mommy! Pineapple!" Karsyn exclaimed. She was standing beside a table full of them jumping up and down.

"Actually, I need two pineapples."

"Can I carry them?" Karsyn grabbed one by the stem and swung it around to Chelsea who barely caught it.

Smiling at Karsyn, Chelsea realized that she didn't remember how "helpful" kids want to be. "You can start. When you get tired, I'll take them." She paid for the pineapples and handed the bag to Karsyn. "You know, when I was in Hawaii a few years ago, I met a couple who lived there. They were sitting on a blanket near the entrance to a park up on a mountain, and they were selling jewelry. They were so happy! Just sitting under the palm trees and talking to people all day long, selling a little of what they were making." She paused as the memory flooded back. Feeling the peace and love in that moment on the mountain made Chelsea smile. "I guess the pineapples reminded me. I had a lot of pineapple in Hawaii. It was so juicy and fresh—"

"I want to go to Hawaii! Can we drive there today?"

The memory felt so reel, but suddenly, she wondered if she really had been there. When did she go? Maybe it was a movie?

Karsyn was looking at her, confused. "Mommy, are you OK?"

"I am ... I don't know when I would have gone to Hawaii. Was I there by myself? Maybe Joss told me about it," Chelsea rushed.

"Maybe it was such a good story that your 'magination told you it was real."

"That has to be it." *How is my kid this wise?*

A short time later, Chelsea and Karsyn dropped off the farmer's market haul at The Salty Cupcake.

"Mommy? I need a snack."

"Of course you do," Chelsea laughed.

"Chocolate chip bagel?"

"That's fine. Let's make it two."

They sat down with their snack, and Karsyn stared sadly at her bagel.

When Chelsea finally noticed, she asked, "What's up Karsyn?" She sipped her coffee and took a bite of the bagel. "Not enough chocolate chips?"

"I'm sad that your memory is broken. I want to fix it."

"Sure, what did you have in mind?"

"I'll tell you about something, and if you remember it, you can talk about it too. Then we can see what you do remember."

"I like that idea. Go ahead. What's first?"

"I remember spending the first night in our townhouse and being scared because I didn't know how Daddy was going to do without us. I thought he would knock on the door in the middle of the night and scare me because he was lonely. Do you remember?"

Chelsea shook her head. "Sorry, I don't."

Karsyn frowned and crossed her arms. "I was really scared. I thought you would remember."

"I don't mean to upset you. I just don't remember that night. Can you be patient with me?"

"OK. Maybe you don't remember because it's a scary memory." Karsyn made monster fingers at Chelsea and then took a bite of her bagel. "What about this. Do you remember the time I rode a pony when I was three?"

Chelsea thought for a moment. "Maybe. Can you tell me a little more?"

"Yes, the pony's name was Sugar, and she was white."

"Do you know where we were for that?"

"Probably near Sugar's house."

"Of course. But was it at a fair? Or a farm?"

"A fair. I bought my mermaid bag there." Karsyn gestured to her favorite messenger bag, which she had slung over the chair when they sat down.

Chelsea tried to picture her sweet daughter a little younger ... that worked! Then she imagined her on a white pony ... but it seemed cartoony. Like she was imagining what that would look like instead of recalling a memory.

"I remember you being there. But I don't remember the pony ride. I guess that's something though."

"It's good Mommy! I'm proud of you!"

Chelsea smiled skeptically at Karsyn. "I'm glad you think that's good. That makes me feel better." Inside, though, she was still concerned. Not much was coming back.

"Maybe now you can tell me stories about you and Aunt Joss when you were little."

"That might help too. You are full of good ideas today!"

"I am. I'm pretty great." They both laughed at that.

"So, when Joss and I were little, we went to a school with funny orange carpet and a big playground. It was right across from a church, and our mom used to park there to wait for us after school. She worked as a dental hygienist in the mornings at a dentist's office nearby so she could always pick us up."

"That's right! Grandma used to clean people's teeth!"

"Good, I got that one! When Joss and I were in second grade, there was a hula hoop contest for the Super Strong Games that our school held every year so all the kids could show off their gym class skills. Joss and I were the final two for the hula hoop contest for our grade, and we both were really competitive. Joss's hoop dropped first, but she grabbed it and tried to keep going. The gym teacher kept blowing the whistle, and she started crying because she lost. I had to hug her and tell her it was OK. And then I shared my ribbon with her. We hung it on the fridge, and I told my parents that we both won."

"Mommy, that's so nice of you!"

"Thanks. I guess we really stuck by each other when we were little." Chelsea took a deep breath and thought about her sister still lying in the hospital bed. *I'm still by your side Joss.*

"Mommy, that's so much memories! I'm excited! It's lots of baby steps, right?"

"That's so sweet, baby. That's something Aunt Joss says. You've been paying attention."

"That's something you say too."

"I do?"

"Yep. I listen to you too." They both laughed.

"You know, I love you so much, and I'm thankful for you every day." Chelsea tried not to cry, but it came anyway. "I just want you to know that, even though you're little, being with you feels like home and everything good in my life wrapped up in one. It would have been so hard to make it through this time without your help, baby."

Karsyn smiled. "Mommy, it's OK to cry. Feelings are good." She popped the last bite of her bagel into her mouth and chewed thoughtfully for a moment while Chelsea pulled a tissue from her purse and wiped her eyes. "Can we walk to the beach to play when we get home?"

Chelsea sniffled and smiled. "Of course."

When they got home, Chelsea and Karsyn packed a picnic for the beach, loaded their wagon, and walked back to the shore. As she pulled the wagon along, something prickled her memory, and she grimaced. She felt pain in her heart that was brought up by pulling the wagon. *When did the two happen together?*

The memory welled up. She was walking to a concert. A sweatshirt tied around her waist. Hair in a ponytail. Long pieces of grass brushed her ankles as she trudged. She wanted to enjoy the atmosphere of joy around her. Everyone was excited for the band ... whoever it was. She couldn't recall that. There beside her was that boyfriend who kept popping up in her fleeting memories. The one who brought that pain to her heart.

"My friends said they didn't want to come because they don't like you, but I don't care what they think."

Chelsea felt her insides shrivel. Was that true? Who says that?

"I don't understand why they don't like me," she muttered.

"Because I want to be around you all the time." He flung an arm over her shoulder and leaned heavily on her. She almost fell backward into the wagon she was pulling.

"Careful."

"Babe, you're good. I got you. You're just clumsy."

The sharpness of his words felt like she was hugging a cactus. "Vic, you almost made me fall." *Ugh, Vic again.*

"Look, you don't have to get in a mood and ruin a good evening. You're lucky that I got us tickets to this. They were sold out, but I knew you wanted to go. You wouldn't believe what I had to do to score these."

"I know. I'm sorry. I appreciate it." She straightened herself, grabbed the handle, and kept pulling the wagon. She glanced at Vic, who laced his hands through the straps of his backpack and marched forward, a self-satisfied gleam in his eye.

"I know you do. No one takes care of you like I do."

Chelsea pulled back from the memory with a shudder and found herself standing completely still in the sand, glazed over, staring at the ocean. She let out a sigh of relief.

"Mommy! Here's a good spot for a picnic!" Karsyn called.

Chelsea shook out of the memory and shuddered again. *I dated that guy? He's clearly a narcissist. Or even a sociopath.* Some things were starting to make sense to her though. The reason she was apprehensive with a relationship for starters. A feeling arose that she had turned off love after she left him, after Joss gave her that sea glass. It must have all changed when she met Damon though. He's a decent guy.

If she skipped over her time with Damon and looked at the relationship with Julian, it made sense that she would be squeamish. But with Adrian ... that was a different story. She felt like she could push aside that dark history to satisfy the craving that was growing like warm, rising bread dough within her.

Gazing again at the ocean, Chelsea breathed in the salt air and pulled the wagon to the spot where Karsyn had started digging. "Are you making a sandcastle?"

"Yes! Can you help me?"

Chelsea flipped out the blanket while Karsyn raced for a bucket of water.

As the afternoon waned, the pair dripped towers of sand all over a mound that Karsyn had piled up. It was so soothing feeling the grit slip through her fingers and watching it form a structure right in front of her. It's amazing how something so simple can build something so beautiful, only to allow the ocean to pull it back to its foundation, when the builder can start afresh and create something totally different.

Maybe that's how life works.

She wondered what it would be like to follow a grain of sand through its transformation from a piece of rock to a speck on the ocean floor to maybe ending up on a beach, trampled every day by beachgoers. And then on to being castle after castle after castle. The hands it must touch. The secrets it must hold. The joy it brings to young and old alike. The imagination and wonder.

A quote she must have loved floated into her mind, bringing with it a feeling of warmth and marvel. "[...] in every curving beach, in every grain of sand, there is the story of the Earth."[1] Who said that? She thought for a moment, and then a name popped up. Of course, environmentalist Rachel Carson. How odd to remember that detail …

Making a mental note to tell Joss about that quote, she wondered if maybe that's where she had heard it originally. It sounded like an idea that would drive a wanderer.

Looking at Karsyn in much the same way she used to look at her sister when they sat on the beach together building castles, she silently wished that Joss could be here to do this with them. Why did she have to push forward on her own? It wasn't fair!

The waves continued to kiss the shore, unaware of the longing and the complicated story playing out nearby.

Chapter Sixteen

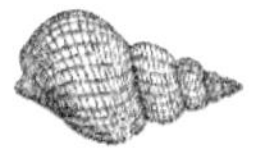

Sunday morning. Karsyn woke Chelsea up by crawling into her bed for snuggles. Chelsea wrapped her arms around her daughter and breathed in the scent of bubblegum shampoo that wafted from her curls. She pulled her close and held her as they just breathed together.

The sun was rising over the Atlantic, painting the clouds with pinks and tangerines. Chelsea could see the clouds from where she lay, but not quite the sea. The building across the street, a strip of shops and restaurants, blocked her view. The light lit the roof of the building, making it glow with warmth. A pair of seagulls landed and then strutted along the roofline. One squawked at the other. Then they flitted away.

"Mommy, what do seagulls say?" Karsyn said.

"I'm not sure. They probably talk about where to find food or a safe place to build a nest. Maybe they warn about predators."

"What do you think those two were saying?"

"One probably said, 'Someone dropped a bagel over there. Want to split it?'" Both of them giggled.

"Can we have breakfast?"

"Sure, baby. You want to get dressed first?"

"Yes. I need a dress today so Aunt Joss can see that I'm fancy."

Chelsea bit her lip. "If she's awake, she will see it, but if she's not, I'm sure she will feel how fancy you are just by your energy."

Karsyn kissed her mommy on the cheek and jumped out of bed, rushing to her room. A few minutes later, the two met in the kitchen. Karsyn had selected a paisley pattern short sleeve dress in pink, blue, and green. She sashayed in and posed.

"Can we make waffles?"

"Yeah, I think we have everything for waffles." Chelsea began pulling out the ingredients, and Karsyn grabbed a bowl and spoon.

"Does Aunt Joss like waffles?" Karsyn stirred the ingredients together, sloshing flour onto the counter.

"She does. But she likes to put syrup on them. I prefer fruit." Chelsea began whipping the egg whites.

"Mommy, I think you like syrup on them too." Karsyn said. She looked at her mother and waited for a response.

"Oh ... maybe I do," Chelsea said. "But today, I feel like putting fruit on them. Can't resist fresh strawberries, right?" She grabbed the strawberries from the fridge and rinsed them.

"Maybe some things changed because of the accident. Maybe you want to be a little different now."

"You might be right," Chelsea said. She chopped up some strawberries as Karsyn folded the egg whites into the waffle mixture, slopping waffle batter over the side of the bowl. *But why can't I remember how I was before? And how can I have an entire life that I only remember from the fringes … after over two weeks?* She smiled at the little girl and began pouring waffle mixture onto the iron, but her thoughts were far away. *How can I keep going like this? How much longer till I'm me?*

After breakfast, Chelsea showered, and the two went to the hospital to see Jocelyn.

A nurse was in the room with her when they arrived. "Good morning! Here to see our sweet Jocelyn?"

"We are," Chelsea responded cheerily. "Any changes?"

The nurse looked at the tablet in her hand. "Nothing really. Her heart rate has remained in the healthy range since it went up a couple days ago, so we are even more optimistic that a change is coming. Her wounds are healing nicely, too. The ribs are looking good. No further internal damage. All in all, she's on the right road for recovery."

"Excuse me, when will she wake up?" Karsyn said. She laid her head against Jocelyn's shoulder and wrapped her arms around hers. Dreamily, she nestled into Jocelyn's hair like she was taking in the whole experience of being near her.

"I can't answer that, dear. It looks good, but I can't make promises, unfortunately."

Chelsea stroked Karsyn's curls. "Hopefully soon. It all sounds pretty positive."

"I agree." The nurse tapped a couple buttons on her tablet screen and then looked up. "I'm on to my next patient. You folks have a good day."

"You too." Chelsea said. She pulled up a chair beside Jocelyn, and Karsyn climbed onto her lap. "Karse, do you want to tell Joss anything about school this week?"

"No. I want to tell her about the castle we made last night. Did you take a picture?"

"I did. I'll find it while you tell her." Chelsea opened her phone and popped up the photo album. It opened in the monthly view, so she could see lots of photos before the castle from yesterday. She clicked on one of her with a man, and when the image opened, she saw that it was Julian. Two days before the accident, they had gotten ice cream and walked along the boardwalk on the southern end of the island, close to Bottle Beach. She barely remembered being at the boardwalk before, but she didn't know when or if anyone was with her. In the picture, their heads were together, and the sunset was in the background.

They looked like two people in love.

Chelsea stared at her face. She looked light as air, but foreign. This was her life before. And it felt so strange to see that everything people were telling her was true. She really was with Julian.

But now ... ?

"Mommy, did you find the picture? I want to show Joss."

"Yes, it's right here." Chelsea slid to the correct picture and handed the phone to Karsyn.

The little girl thrust the phone toward Jocelyn's face. "This is the castle we built. It was so gigantic! See all the towers? There are like a million of them. Mommy is pretty good at castles."

"So are you, cupcake," Chelsea chimed in.

Karsyn grinned and continued chattering about the castle and who should live there.

Chelsea gazed at her sister, who remained motionless except for her slow, peaceful breathing. In and out. In and out. Just like the tides. She closed her eyes too. If she listened carefully, she could just hear the sound of Jocelyn's breath. On that sound, she let herself wander into a meditation.

On a beach, where she felt comfortable to imagine herself, she pictured herself sitting cross-legged in the sand. The ocean lapped to the rhythm of Jocelyn's breathing. As she took in the scene in her mind's eye, she asked the Universe to send her some recent memories so she could start piecing things together and get back to whatever she had before. Everything was ill-fitting.

Ill-fitting ... like the boots Zara was trying to put on. My life doesn't fit right. I need more information so I can feel like I am back in my own shoes. That constant discomfort of wondering what I am going to say or do next because it might not be something that "Chelsea" normally did ... it was aggravating! Hey, Universe, can you help me?

In her mind's eye, she felt the nudge to look right and saw a huge piece of green sea glass protruding from the sand.

I know that. I already brought some to Joss. And I know Joss gave me some when I broke up with Vic. What else?

Her request was met with the steady rise and fall of the waves, echoing Jocelyn's breathing again.

As they left the hospital a few minutes later, Chelsea's phone buzzed. She pulled it out, in case it was Damon.

It was a text from Julian.

"Hi Chelse, just wanted to see how your weekend is going."

It would be rude not to respond right away.

"Pretty good. Took care of some stuff for the shop and hung out with Karsyn. We just visited Joss. It was nice. How was yours?"

"Good. Read a little bit at the beach, cleaned the house, biked across to the mainland."

"Nice! By the way, I appreciate that you've been giving me some space. Can we just keep it to texting this week and see how things go?"

"We can."

Chelsea put her phone away and helped Karsyn into the car. She let out a sigh of relief, realizing that she had been holding her breath while she texted Julian. Always holding her breath.

How long should I do this before I'm certain of what to do? And what do I do about Adrian?

Her stomach fluttered at the thought and then settled again.

And did I always hold my breath before ...

Chapter Seventeen

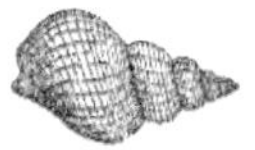

The beach was covered in a thick fog. It felt like mist on her skin. Chelsea shivered in her thin, strappy romper. *Where is my sweater?* The cold soaked to her core.

Though the sky was getting light, the sun was nowhere to be seen. Walking on the beach felt more like wandering in a cloud of damp white blankets. Chelsea's toes pressed into the soggy sand as she navigated the sweet spot where the surf caressed the shore. Foam popped on the sand as the tide retreated. Still, she walked.

Where am I going?

Ahead, a form emerged from the fog, matching her height and gait. Just to their left, another walked through the water, sloshing gently with each step.

The three met a few feet apart and stopped. The fog began lifting from them, forming a protective bubble around their council.

Chelsea gazed at Jocelyn and Zara. "Here we are again." But this felt like a dream rather than a gathering of sister souls. Both of the other women stared ahead with blank faces. Robotic. Emotionless.

Suddenly, she knew she had to check on the elephant. "We don't have an elephant. This is ridiculous."

Still, the three ventured back into the fog in search of an elephant.

Chelsea was suddenly in a kitchen, opening a box by the sink. She felt like she was unpacking in a new home. She removed a few delicate teacups and placed them in a cupboard. Then, she unwrapped a bundle of tissue paper in the bottom of the box. It was a ruby elephant, about the size of her hand, with a long pink tassel dangling from its belly. Standing on tiptoe, she hung the elephant above the sink and felt instant relief, as if her mission were complete. Sunlight twinkled through the elephant as it danced in the light breeze from the open window. Pink light bounced around the room.

She stepped back and gazed at it for a moment before she felt that she was in her own bedroom, gazing out the window. Turning, she saw that she wasn't alone. "Zara."

Zara motioned toward the nightstand and touched the front of the drawer. In the dream, Chelsea followed her and pulled the drawer open. Inside was a collection of children's toys that she would classify as junk. Little plastic prizes from the local pizza palace, bracelets, tiny notepads ... and sticking out of the pile was the corner of a notebook.

Chelsea put both hands in the drawer but couldn't seem to find the notebook that she just saw. Frustrated, she pulled the drawer out and dumped it.

The little toys scattered everywhere, but the drawer never seemed to empty. She continued to shake it. Bits and baubles fell and chinked across the floor. The noise sounded like the roar of ocean waves. Finally, Chelsea dropped the drawer and yanked out the bottom one. It was completely empty. She got down on her hands and knees on top of the huge pile and tried to reach her arm under the nightstand, but she couldn't get to it. It was always out of reach no matter how she moved.

Anger surged through her, and she turned to look for Zara for help. She was gone.

As she stood, Chelsea found herself back on the beach, listening to the waves, staring out at the fog as it enveloped her like a thick blanket. The weight, like a thousand worries, sunk her shoulders and pulled her down toward the sand until she collapsed on her knees. Her hand brushed the ground in front of her, and there, sticking out of the sand, was the corner of that notebook.

"This is a ridiculous dream," Chelsea said. She shook herself awake. Feelings of frustration, confusion, overwhelm, and exhaustion tangled together and formed a web through her brain. Puffing up her pillow, she frowned, rolled onto her side, and forced all the thoughts away. *Sleep.*

When the harp played, Chelsea rolled onto her back and opened her eyes. The sun shown again.

What happened?

Most mornings, she awoke refreshed and feeling joy, but today ... there was fear. Trepidation. Uncertainty.

Chelsea sat up, stretched, and rolled her shoulders, hoping to shake off the funk. She grabbed her water bottle from the nightstand and took a long drink. As she put it back, the feeling washed over her again.

The nightstand.

Her entire dream came back. The beach. The red elephant. Zara. The notebook.

What did that all mean? Do I really have a notebook?

Feeling a little silly about it, Chelsea pulled open the top drawer of the nightstand, fully expecting to see socks or sweatshirts or something else she forgot she put in there. The only thing in that drawer, though, was a notebook.

For a moment, she stared at it, not sure what was in it. Then, she gingerly picked it up and gave the cover a full once-over. It was obnoxious pink with bright green watercolor palm trees. In gold lettering across the front was the sentence "Do brave things."

Glancing out the window, Chelsea recalled the dream. That book must be important. But why? And what was she doing that was "brave"?

"Mommy?"

Chelsea turned and saw a tiny blond bedhead peeking at her on the other side of the mattress. "Yes baby?"

"Will you braid my hair for school today?"

"Of course." Chelsea replaced the book in the drawer. She had important things to do, so figuring out what she was writing in there would have to wait.

When the bus came, Karsyn hopped on, French-braided pigtails bouncing along behind her—yes, Chelsea's fingers somehow remembered how to French braid. Chelsea felt her heart surge as Karsyn turned and waved at her on the top step. The little girl grinned, jumped into the seat with a friend, and waved out the window. The bus rolled down the street.

Something about being that little girl's mother took her breath away. Chelsea wondered if she had paused to think much about it before the accident. That accident easily could have taken her from Karsyn, but here she was—still breathing, still loving her, still raising her to be a powerful, kind adult.

Hopefully.

She climbed into her car and sat for a moment before starting it. What a strange thing it is to be a mother. Feeling all that love and the energy of her daughter wrapped up tight in that little package was enough to bring the tears if she let it. It had been fairly easy the past few days, with Damon's and Megan's and Samantha's help, but she knew that Karsyn had also been on her best behavior. Helping her in the kitchen, reminding her of things, picking up her toys just before she asked her to ... For five years old, Karsyn had done incredibly well.

It was so strange to feel this kind of love and need to protect another human from everything and yet send her off into the world every day to figure it out on her own. Part of her wanted to chase down the bus and pull the little one back into her arms before letting her go again. Maybe this evening they would do something special together, just mommy and daughter. The whole world revolves around that tiny smile.

Pulling herself back to the present moment, Chelsea realized that tears were rolling down her face and that she needed to head to work. She felt an urge to run back in the house and grab the notebook and read it, but she should get moving.

She smiled and dabbed a tissue on her cheeks. What a life she had woken up to. To feel at home and loved and blissful and also to feel off-kilter and confused ... what a strange combination of emotions.

Rooting herself in the love she had for Karsyn and her desire to set herself back on the right course so she could create a stable home and loving place for Karsyn to be—because that's what a mother should do—she buckled her seatbelt and pulled into the street.

This was home, and it was starting to feel more that way. Maybe that was a good sign.

Chapter Eighteen

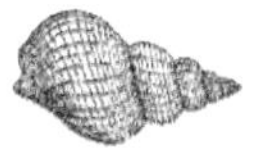

The Salty Cupcake was buzzing with activity when Chelsea arrived.

In the back, Isabel, Kelli, and Erika were baking, while Samantha and Maisie were working the cash registers.

"We're pretty busy for a Monday!" Chelsea said.

"There is a book and arts festival in the park this week." Samantha tipped her head in the direction of the park, about a block away. "It will probably be crazy every morning. It's like this every year," she whispered loudly over the din.

"Really?" Chelsea frowned. No memory of a festival in the park. Surely, she had gone before. It sounded so fun! "This is getting insane," she muttered as she pushed back through the door into the kitchen. Glancing at the board, she saw a substantial list of needs, so she erased one and got started.

Cinnamon biscotti ... I don't remember making this, but surely, I have before. She frowned again. *Why isn't this getting easier?*

Gathering the ingredients, Chelsea found a workstation and started dumping and mixing. As she did, the ideas in her head started churning as well.

*What is in that notebook? What is brave? Why do I need to **tell** myself to be brave?*

Is it new? Or old? It can't be old-old, or I would probably remember it, since I remember most of the stuff from a long time ago.

Oh no, what if I'm sick? What if there is something wrong with me and THAT'S why I had a miscarriage?

Chelsea ripped her attention from her thoughts and focused on the biscotti. *This is going nowhere. Why am I coming up with crazy scenarios? Maybe I just liked the cover.*

As she flattened the biscotti into logs, Chelsea realized that she does brave things every day. Maybe it was nothing to worry about. Really. But she still itched to read what was inside. She placed the logs into the oven for the first bake and leaned against the counter.

Her thoughts returned to her constant conundrum, Julian and Adrian. *Maybe I don't need to figure this out either. Maybe it will just naturally unfold. I've been gifted with two amazing men in my life, but I'm recovering from a car wreck. My memory isn't even back yet! Maybe I can just give this all to the Universe and let it sort itself out. Like throwing that biscotti in the oven. We will see what comes of it.*

Hopefully biscotti comes out of the oven.

She shrugged and sent her worries to the oven of the Universe. *Give them back when there is something for me to go on. Or eat.*

Why is my brain going so hard on all my problems today? How about back to Karsyn ... what should we do this evening?

Chelsea cleaned up her workspace while she waited for the first bake of the biscotti. She loaded the dishwasher and wiped down the counter. The others in the kitchen rotated between their baking and cleaning up tasks as well. For all the noise on the other side of the door, the kitchen was fairly calm and quiet.

"Cookie for your thoughts?" Samantha had appeared at her elbow with a Chocolate Treasure cookie, fresh from the oven.

"I wasn't thinking about cookies, but now I am," Chelsea took the cookie and nibbled a bite.

"You look like you have a lot on your mind."

"Always. Also, nothing, apparently. I'm not making any progress on my memory."

"It's not something you can force. You have to be open to your memories returning and relax. I doubt stress will make them come back any faster."

"I know. I've been focusing on other things ... but those other things are a little stressful."

"I'm sure." Samantha finished her cookie and washed her hands. "Still not sure what to do about your man problem?"

"Why do you call it a 'man problem'? That makes me sound like a sleaze."

"No it doesn't. It makes you sound popular." Samantha chuckled and peeked in the oven at the biscotti. "So, do you know what you're going to do yet? Are you still talking to Julian?"

Chelsea finished her cookie too. "It's complicated." Then she peeked at the biscotti too. "I'm just going to let it play out and go with my gut."

"That sounds good. It's probably best that way. You don't want to overthink love."

"You know it's easier to say that when you're not the one in the middle of it," Chelsea gave her a wry look.

"True!" Samantha shrugged. "I'm going back to the front." She pushed through the door into the restaurant.

As the oven buzzed, Chelsea donned oven mitts and removed the tray of biscotti. *I suppose I have been overthinking the whole thing. Maybe it would be best to take a break from both of them for a couple days.* She sliced up the biscotti and flipped it over on the tray. *Clearing my head is a good idea anyway. Sam is right. Stress will keep my memory from coming back.* Sliding the tray back into the oven, Chelsea let out a deep breath. *Time to focus on me. And on Karsyn. Just what's important.*

A short ten minutes later, and Chelsea was pulling the biscotti back out of the oven.

"Those smell amazing," Erika said.

"They really do," Chelsea agreed. She breathed in deeply and felt herself relax as the blend of cinnamon and fresh baked cookies brought peace to her soul. *How lucky am I that this is my life?* Finally starting to feel like things were normal and she belonged would surely help with the memory problem.

She moved the biscotti to a rack and grabbed a display tray for them. When they were cool, Chelsea transferred the cookies to the tray. With tray in hand, she backed into the door to the restaurant to push it open and turned to face the room.

"Excellent. I thought they would be out soon," Samantha said. "Someone is waiting on a cinnamon biscotti."

Of course! Chelsea's face reddened. She raised her eyebrows and slid the tray into its spot in the display. "Good morning! How are you today?"

Adrian approached the counter and smiled. He leaned on the case like he couldn't get close enough to her. "Good morning yourself! I'm great now that my biscotti is ready. Can't have a good day without it, right?"

"Oh, you probably could, but it would take a lot of sunshine and little kids singing 'Happy birthday!' to make up for it," Chelsea responded.

He chuckled. "Probably way more than the recommended dose of both of those. I'll just stick with the biscotti."

"A wise choice." Chelsea laughed too.

"So how was your weekend?"

"It was nice. I took my daughter to the farmer's market on Saturday and then saw my sister at the hospital on Sunday."

"The farmer's market here is the best. I was there Saturday too with my niece and nephew. They like it when I take them there because they know Uncle Adrian is going to spoil them."

"That's so sweet. How old are they?"

"Eight and ten. My sister always appreciates a morning when she and her husband can have their coffee and quiet, so I pop over and get the kids for that on occasion."

Chelsea's heart fluttered. "That's so nice of you."

"It's not all innocent. I know I get ice cream if I take them, and it's more fun having a cone with the kids because you get to try everyone's ice cream."

"Of course. I do the same with my daughter."

"How old is she?"

"She'll be six in July. She talks like she's an adult, though. So clever sometimes."

"I know what you mean. Are you guys traveling any this summer?"

Chelsea looked at Samantha for a moment, but she wasn't going to help. She was taking an order. "Honestly, I don't know. I need to look through my stuff and see what I have planned. I haven't found a planner. There isn't one on my phone. And I just don't remember. You would think I would be excited if I had a trip planned, so I'm guessing I don't."

Adrian smiled sympathetically. "So, you're not remembering things any better?"

"Just some of my childhood." Chelsea recalled the vivid memories of Vic. "It seems like everything I remember was a big imprint on my brain, like major events, things that were really important to me. But then my life as an adult is almost like photographs. I only remember little snippets." She leaned her chin on her hands on top of the case.

"Well, maybe as you start making new memories, the old ones will start to come back," he looked importantly at her, as if he were about to say something else.

Chelsea's heart thundered in her chest. *Is he going to ask me out? He can't ask me out. But I want him to! I want to say "yes"! I want to stare into those eyes forever!* Her thoughts hammered through her brain at the same pace as her heartbeat. Chelsea bit her lip. "I'm sure that's true." She lowered her eyes shyly. *Shyly? I'm not shy! What the heck is going on?*

Adrian reached across the case and touched her hand lightly. Electricity sizzled through Chelsea's body. "I was wondering if maybe we could grab coffee sometime. I love talking to you. I'd like to get to know you better."

Chelsea glanced at Samantha, who was pouring a cup of coffee nearby, and saw her raise her eyebrows and smile. The customers had dwindled while they talked. She turned back to Adrian. "You know, I would love to do that, but you only get coffee here. Everyone would be watching us."

Adrian glanced back at Samantha and started laughing. "I see your point. How about a drink? There is a beautiful winery on the mainland, not too far from here."

I should say "no." "Um." *Good grief Chelsea.* Her heart raced.

"Maybe this Friday?" Adrian pulled out his phone. "They have an acoustic jazz guitar player performing that night, so it's a nice atmosphere. I was planning on going just to listen, but it would be nice to have company."

"That sounds really nice," Chelsea said. She felt the heat rising in her face again as she thought about whether she really should say "no." Then her hand tingled again where he had touched her, and she shoved the feeling of guilt away. But then again ... "You know, I might have Karsyn this Friday, though."

"Can I get your number?" He handed her his phone. "Then you can just let me know."

Chelsea took the phone and paused. *What's my phone number?* "Funny. I, uh, can't remember my phone number."

He laughed. "I've never heard that excuse before. Could I give you mine?"

Chelsea paused. "Yeah. That will work." She pulled out her phone and handed it to him. He typed his name and number, and she immediately texted him.

Adrian's phone dinged. "Got it."

Chelsea took a deep breath and smiled nervously. "I do want to be honest with you." *But not too honest, right Chelse?* "I'm still trying to get my feet under me since the car wreck. And I would really like to hang out. But I don't know that I'm ready for anything right now. I know that's really weird, but it's just my headspace for the time being." *That wasn't really a "no," Chelsea.*

"I understand. No pressure." Adrian put his phone back in his pocket. "I *am* looking forward to Friday, though. I hope you can join me." He reached across the counter and touched her hand again, and she felt another surge of electricity. Then he smiled, and her heart melted.

For a moment, the world stood still as Chelsea just enjoyed the heat of his hand on hers and lost herself in his beautiful amber-brown eyes. She didn't even notice the door to the shop open and usher in more than just another customer.

Chapter Nineteen

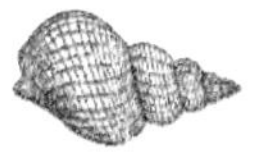

"Chelsea?"

Her blood froze in her veins. Startled, she jerked her hand back from the counter. "Julian. Hi."

Adrian looked at Julian and then back at Chelsea. From the look on his face, he didn't realize the significance of his ill timing. "I'll talk to you later!" He waved at Chelsea and then walked out the door with his coffee and biscotti.

I wonder what he saw. Chelsea glanced down guiltily at her hands and then fiddled with the door on the case as if it didn't close properly.

"Was that guy bothering you?" Julian approached the counter and looked incredulous. "Do you want me to say something?"

"He's a friend," Chelsea said. "He was just asking about Joss." She acted busy, checked the coffee pots, refilled napkins. Samantha had conveniently disappeared into the kitchen. "Did it look like he was bothering me?"

"I've never seen him before," Julian said. He still sounded suspicious. "I saw him touching your hand, and I wasn't sure what he was doing."

Chelsea reddened as rage coursed through her. "You don't *own* me, Julian. I can have friends."

"That's not at all what I meant. He just ... the way he looked at you." Julian sighed and ran a hand through his hair. "I just wanted to make sure you're OK."

Chelsea glanced out the front window and realized that Adrian must be thinking the same thing. He had sat down at one of the tables and was slowly dipping his biscotti in his coffee, giving cautious sideways glances through the shop window. *Good grief.*

"I'm fine." *Now I have to make sure that Adrian gets out of here before Julian sees him watching him. I don't know if he's the kind of guy who will confront him. Why do I feel guilty about this? I asked Julian to give me space?* "What are you doing here?"

"I wanted a coffee and thought I would support my favorite bakery," Julian said. He pulled out his wallet.

Do I actually make my boyfriend pay for his coffee? "You don't have to do that." She waved his money away. "What kind?"

"Dark roast."

"Do you want room for cream and sugar?" *I should tell him we need a break to make myself clear ...*

Julian laughed. "You still don't remember?"

Chelsea's face flushed again. Then she firmly said, "Look, I've been confused and frustrated and everything else since the accident. I still don't even remember you, OK. Sorry. I'm not going to remember your coffee order." She put her hands over her face and bit her lip trying to hold back the tears.

"Geez, Chelse, I didn't mean it like that. I was just joking. I know you don't remember this stuff."

Chelsea almost suggested that he leave when she saw Adrian staring in the window at her. *Shit.* She shook her hands and glanced at the ceiling. *Can I get a break here, Universe?* "Look, I'm just a little emotional today. Let's sit and talk for a minute. Do you want a bagel or something?"

"Sure. An everything bagel if you have one left."

Chelsea was still fuming as she grabbed the bagel from the case, poured herself a coffee, and grabbed a raspberry scone. She herded Julian to the coffee station and then a table far from the door, hoping that he wouldn't notice that Adrian was still out there.

"Joss hasn't changed at all. She's still doing well, healing. But they aren't seeing any sign of her coming out of the coma soon." She was talking fast. "It's been well over two weeks, and I'm stressed about it. I have always been so close with her. It's like not being able to talk to your best friend. She's been there since before I was born, you know."

"I'm not going to pretend to know what you're going through, but I know you're scared. I'm here for you." Julian reached across the table and touched Chelsea's hand.

She recoiled, put her hand on her lap, and stared blankly at the scone in front of her.

Julian sat back in his chair. "I know you wanted space. I miss you. I thought it would be OK to pop in and get a coffee and just say 'hi.' If that's not OK, then just tell me."

Nervously, Chelsea glanced at the table outside. Adrian must have slipped away when she looked down.

Julian turned and looked at the door. "What are you looking at?"

"A bird landed on that table outside."

"Are you sure that guy wasn't bothering you? You seem really shaken up."

"You know, right now, YOU are bothering me. I asked for a little space to pull my life back together after a major car accident, and you just won't listen."

"God, Chelsea, you're my girlfriend. *I love you.* We had our future laid out in front of us. Now it's like we're total strangers." Julian stared at her, eyes wide, like he was surprised.

"Look, I can't argue with you in here. Let's step outside for a minute. Then I need to get back to the kitchen."

"If that's what you want, fine."

Now I pushed him too far ... Maybe that's what I want? Chelsea grabbed her coffee and scone and set them on the case. Then she steered Julian out the front door. *Should I really just ask for a break?* Something inside of her was scared to, like she was still the little girl that Vic shoved around.

The pair stood in front of the shop, staring emptily at each other, Chelsea with her hands on her hips and Julian clutching his coffee and bagel like they were a consolation prize.

"Chelsea, I know you hurt, but I hurt too. I just want you to be aware of that."

Chelsea swallowed hard and took a deep, calming breath. "My head has been cloudy. And I don't understand what's going on half the time. I keep looking around trying to find clues to my past life. I looked at pictures of us in my phone, and I still don't even remember being with you before."

"I don't get it," Julian shook his head. "I mean I do, but I don't. I don't know why your memory isn't coming back. And I don't know why it feels so different for us now. I haven't felt like you were your normal self since the accident. It's like you have a huge icy wall up. I want to get us back to the place where we were. I'm just ... confused."

"*You're* confused?" Chelsea threw her hands up. "How do you think I feel? I wake up to this strange life one day, and everyone just expects me to jump right back in."

"Look, I didn't come here to get into an argument," Julian said. "I'll just go. We can talk another time. I'm sorry I upset you so much."

"Thank you. I need space. As I said." *And a break? Maybe?* She bit her lip as she watched him, nervous about how far she had pushed him. Nervous about what type of person he really was ... she totally didn't remember. It was like walking on eggshells trying to ask for what she wants and deciding if she should just push him away till he said enough.

Or is that what she wants at all?

Julian started to walk away and then looked back at her. Fuming, he shook his head and continued to his car.

Chelsea continued to glare in his direction with her arms crossed until he backed out and drove away.

Chapter Twenty

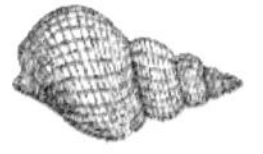

That's when the tears fell.

Chelsea stood there in the mid-morning sun, looking out at the parking lot, standing in front of the bakery that she built with her love and dreams of a better life, and sobbed.

The overwhelm of the past two weeks flowed freely from her, and she sank down into a seat at one of the café tables outside. Laying her head on her arms, she sighed. Her throat tight, her nose stuffy, her eyes burning, she cried.

A moment later, someone else touched her hand. "Chelse?" she whispered.

"Zara?" she sniffed.

"It's Sam." Samantha gently stroked her arm. "I'm here for you, hon."

Chelsea tipped her head up and propped her chin on her arms. "I'm tired of being strong."

"I know." She said gently. Then she handed Chelsea a tissue and stroked her arm lovingly.

The friends sat in silence for several minutes.

"Do you think that this is part of my soul journey?" Chelsea finally said.

"I think that's way too complicated to think about right now."

Chelsea gazed across the street at the ocean. A gull screamed overhead. A couple walked in the sand, laughing and holding hands. A little boy yelled excitedly about a blue truck that drove by.

"It amazes me that our little problems always make the world feel like it's caving in, but then you look around, and everything is still going."

Samantha looked out at the ocean too. "I know. It's funny how things work like that."

For a moment, they both watched the waves. In and out. In and out.

"Do you suppose I'll ever get my memory back?"

"If you don't, you can always make new memories. Humans are resilient like that."

"What if I veered off course?"

"It doesn't take a car wreck to do that. We all veer off course from time to time." Samantha leaned back and crossed her ankles. "But then, you have to wonder if that was the course we were meant to take after all. Everything has its season."

Chelsea smiled weakly at Samantha. "Thanks for being here for me."

"What are friends for?" Samantha reached across the table and squeezed Chelsea's hand. Chelsea squeezed back. "Did you want to talk about what happened?"

"Not really." Chelsea sniffed. "I don't really know myself what happened. I might have just chased Julian away."

"If Julian is anything, he's loving, patient, and kind. I've seen all of that when I've been around you guys. You were happy together. I wouldn't count him out just yet."

"It's a shame I can't decide if I *want* to count him out or not."

"You don't need to make a decision today." Samantha stood. "But ... you do need to make some cupcakes."

Chelsea laughed. "True."

"How about Joss's favorite? What does she like?"

"Tropical punch."

"Maybe she'll smell them and wake up. Come on." She grabbed Chelsea's hand and pulled her back in the restaurant. "Jada, take the front for a while. I'm going to make cupcakes with Chelsea."

Jada finished tying her apron and gave a thumbs up. She wiped down the counter as Chelsea and Samantha pushed through the door into the kitchen.

Wiping her face with a tissue, Chelsea breathed in deeply. The smell of fresh baked goodies wafted around her like a protective quilt. *This is where I belong.* "Sam, you want to grab the butter and eggs?"

"I'd love to."

The pair pulled out the ingredients, and Chelsea erased "Random cupcakes" off of the list for the day.

Samantha poured out the dry ingredients while Chelsea creamed the butter and sugar. Then she chopped some pineapple, cut a passionfruit, and scooped the pulp and seeds out. And she mixed both into the wet ingredients.

"Joss would love these," Chelsea said. Her eyes watered again. *I guess today is a crying day. Once you break the seal ...*

Samantha smiled.

It feels so comfortable to just bake and be with the creation. Hey Universe, help me out, and bring Joss back. We need to be together, and I need her to help figure out my life. We are used to leaning on each other.

Samantha began lining pans with their signature pink and white cupcake papers. As she tipped the mixer into the batter, Chelsea realized that she would have Karsyn that evening. *Thank goodness!* At least she would have something to focus on, so she didn't go crazy thinking about the drama from today.

"Oh!" Chelsea suddenly said.

"You OK?" Samantha glanced at the knife she was cleaning.

Chelsea held up the knife and laughed. "I'm good. Just remembered that I found my journal this morning."

"I take it that's good."

"Not sure. I didn't get to read any of it."

"Maybe tonight?"

"I should have time. I have Karsyn tonight, but I can at least see what's in there. Maybe it will give me some reminders of the past that will kick start my memory."

"Keep me in the loop. I know you've been patient, but it would be nice if this stirred something up."

"I agree."

After an uneventful afternoon, Chelsea hopped in her car to meet Karsyn at the bus stop. She got home fifteen minutes ahead of the bus and jogged up the stairs to her bedroom. Pulling the journal from the nightstand, she flipped through a few pages just to judge the timeframe as she meandered back toward the front door.

Aunt Dana texted just then to check on her, and Chelsea sent her a quick message letting her know that she was doing fine. Then she eagerly dove into the journal.

"Here's April 19th ... 'I can't believe I lost him. He wasn't with us very long, but still. I love him. Julian is devastated too. This would have been his first child. Annie said that writing about it would help, but not much. I still feel this emptiness.'"

"What the hell?" she said aloud. Chelsea pushed through the front door. *That was only about a month ago* ... Sitting on the bench on the porch, she closed the book on her thumb and sank into her thoughts. *Do I feel empty? I don't think I do. Should I? How can I not even remember that little life?* She flipped the book open to the next page.

"'We decided that Julian will meet my family at our birthday party. Joss will be so thrilled to meet him! I hate keeping him a secret, but I had to make sure that I was ready for Karsyn to meet him. Sometimes, I can't believe I was so scared, even with the baby, to let Karsyn meet him, but I just wasn't ready. I am now. I feel better. More alive. More together and certain of where my life is going than I've ever been. And Julian is wonderful! I've never met anyone like him. He's definitely my soulmate.'"

Chelsea frowned. "Soulmate? Seriously?" *Not sure about that one. And isn't it ironic to write that I was so certain of my path and then find myself here a few weeks later ...*

She flipped a few more pages forward to the week of the accident. "'I can hardly stand it! I'm so excited for Joss to meet Julian! She's going to love him! Karsyn will too. I know he loves kids, and meeting Karsyn will be so perfect, especially since we want to move in together.'"

Chelsea closed the book and tossed it on the bench beside her. She pulled her knees up and wrapped her arms around her legs. "WTF. For real. We were having a baby and talking about living together? And I don't even feel attracted to him. Am I numb? Am I scared? Or is this a big 'no'?" She bit her lip. *I just don't think that's right! It's not fear. It's just not for me.*

The grumble of a bus's engine down the street called Chelsea's attention to the road. Karsyn would be home in a minute. She shook her hands at the sky. Then she closed her eyes and took three deep centering breaths. *Karsyn can't see me like this. I have to be a good mom.* When she opened her eyes, the bus was pulling up to the block of townhouses.

Karsyn bounced off the bus and into Mommy's arms.

"Hello, sunshine! Did you have a good day?"

"So good, Mommy! We had a guest who plays the trumpet in a band, and she was so cool. And loud!"

Chelsea laughed. "Of course she was!" She grabbed the journal off the bench, and the two went inside. "I thought we could walk to the beach this evening. Maybe have a picnic. I brought home cupcakes."

"Yay! What kind?"

"Tropical punch. Joss's favorite." She smiled weakly.

Karsyn frowned. "Is she going to come home soon?"

"I thought maybe if I made her favorite cupcakes, she might."

Chelsea packed the cupcakes and some waters in their cooler, and the pair got ready for the beach. They loaded the wagon and crossed the street.

Watching Karsyn splash in the waves was soothing. She's so free and joyful. Living in the moment. Doing whatever she feels. Kicking the water, jumping over waves, running into the water and back out. Finally, she decided that she was hungry, so Chelsea got out their snacks.

They listened to the waves crashing. A pair of gulls landed nearby and bravely cried for a bite. "This is my cupcake, seagulls. You can't have it," Karsyn said. Chelsea laughed.

The cupcakes were divine. Super moist. Chunks of fruit. Karsyn had never tried them before, but she clearly loved them. Hers was gone in an instant. "I know why this is Aunt Joss's favorite." She ran her teeth over the cupcake wrapper to get as much cake as possible till Chelsea stopped her.

"You ready to splash?" Chelsea said.

Karsyn leaped up and ran back to the ocean. Chelsea followed, and the two were silly together kicking the water and giggling.

"Mommy, look," Karsyn said. She ran over to a chunk of sea glass sticking out of the sand. When she picked it up, it fit in the palm of her hand.

"How did you see that?"

"I have super vision."

"You must." Chelsea looked at Karsyn's treasure. It was flat and square-ish. "You know, when I was in Spain, I went in a shop where they had the most beautiful mosaic tables made with glass like this. Greens and blues on some tables. Reds and yellows on others. So many striking patterns and designs. There was one with an octopus and fish and other sea creatures that I wanted so badly, but I had nowhere to put it because I was renting apartments wherever I went at the time. I can clearly see it ..." Chelsea gazed off, lost in the memory.

"Mommy?" Karsyn said. "Where is Spain? Can we go?"

Glancing back at her daughter, Chelsea suddenly froze. *When was I in Spain? Was it a couple years ago? But Karsyn is five. Did I have her with me? Who takes a toddler halfway around the world? Isn't that where I met that man from Canada and kissed him on the roof? Am I going crazy? But that table ... I remember it so clearly ... There's no way Karsyn could have been with me.* She stared at Karsyn wide-eyed. *It had to be a movie. Or maybe I'm remembering one of Joss's stories.*

"Mommy … are you OK?"

"I'm … I'm fine. I just. Wow. I think Joss told me about that … but no … no, it was *my* memory. I *know* it was mine."

Karsyn started crying. "Mommy? Mommy, you're scaring me."

"It's OK, cupcake. It's scary for me too, but I'm starting to remember some things. Maybe I was in Spain a long time ago. I can flip through the albums at the house and find it. When we get home, I'll look."

Chelsea tried to scoop her up, but Karsyn pushed away.

"You're not my mommy!" Karsyn balled her fists and stood her ground. "You smell weird."

Chapter Twenty-One

"I smell weird?" Chelsea knelt so they were eye-to-eye. Her heart was pounding. There was something about what Karsyn had said ...

"Yes!" Karsyn threw her hands up, frustrated. "You haven't smelled right since that wreck. I think it messed up your smell *and* your memory. You haven't been my mommy since I got you back from the hospital!"

"Wow, am I that different?" Chelsea sat heavily in the sand. Her head was swimming. *It isn't just my memory? Something might be really wrong ...*

"I just want my old mommy back!" Karsyn yelled. She tromped back to their picnic site, grabbed a bucket, and then ran off to the ocean and filled the bucket with water.

I didn't realize it was so upsetting for her. How can I fix this? Chelsea's eyes filled with tears as she stared after her daughter, who was dipping the bucket into the sea. *Of course it's been rough on her. Her mom doesn't remember much of her life at all, and she's the most important person on this planet!*

Karsyn approached Chelsea with the bucket and a dour face. "Mommy, I'm going to fix your memory. I can't fix your smell because I'm not a scientist, but I know I can fix your memory."

Surprised, Chelsea nodded. "OK, that sounds … wonderful. I really appreciate you working on this with me. I know it's important to you that I get my memory back. What's your new plan?"

"I'll show you when we get home." Karsyn turned back to the sandcastle and began adding more towers to it.

"I can't wait." Chelsea joined her for a while, adding more towers and wondering what that little head had cooked up.

When the castle was deemed complete a short time later, Chelsea loaded the wagon as Karsyn emptied the sand from her toys. She was curious to see if Karsyn could help her memory. Surely something would work … soon. The walked back home, pulling the wagon. Chelsea was pensive. Karsyn looked determined.

After baths, Chelsea and Karsyn met in their pajamas in the living room.

"What's the plan?" Chelsea asked.

"It's simple," Karsyn answered. "Let's look at pictures, and I'll tell you stories." She grabbed a photo album from the shelf by the TV.

"Maybe it will work this time," Chelsea said cautiously. "I tried looking at a couple already, and nothing really looked familiar."

"This is from before I was born. It's really old. Let's try this first."

"'Really old,' huh?" Chelsea chuckled. "Let's give it a shot."

Flipping the book open, Karsyn placed it on Chelsea's lap and sank onto the couch beside her. "This is a picture from when you first opened the bakery. There's Aunt Jocelyn and Samantha and some of the other people who worked there then."

Touching the picture, Chelsea grinned. "Wow, eight years ago. That looks so old. Look at my hair ..." She touched her own hair and marveled at how much her hair had changed over the years.

"Look at Joss's!" Karsyn crinkled her nose. "It's black."

"It *is* black ... I remember ..." Chelsea frowned as some thoughts collided in her head. Something strange about that moment ... "I remember how I felt. Something doesn't seem right. I was happy, but I was also sad."

"That's good! You remember something!" Karsyn said. "Anything else?" Chelsea shook her head, so Karsyn flipped back a few pages to another picture. "This is when you and Daddy were in love." She pointed at Chelsea and Damon snuggling by a fire pit. A few friends sat nearby.

Chelsea closed her eyes and focused on the feeling. "Nothing. Sorry."

Karsyn flipped forward a few pages. "This is you and Aunt Joss and Grandma. It's when Grandma was sick, so Aunt Joss came back to see her before she passed."

"That I remember! We took Mom to get apple pie at her favorite restaurant on the Cape. We drove for an hour, and she started feeling sick, so we had to pull over till she felt OK again. We sat by the beach and watched a couple kids playing with their dog, and Mom said it reminded her of what she loved so much about life." Chelsea's eyes filled with tears.

"What did Grandma like?"

"Freedom and love and playing. She said that if she came back to this planet, she wanted to be a dog in a house with kids because she thought they were some of the most loved creatures with the most fabulous lifestyles. We were all laughing so hard as she described how she would lay around in the sun and let the kids dress her up in doll clothes. Mom was panting like a dog and putting her 'paws' up in the air. It was one of the funniest memories I have of her. She was always making us laugh, but that was so precious."

Karsyn was quiet for a moment, and then she asked, "Did Grandma get her apple pie?"

"She did. After we all laughed, we felt better. She said her stomach stopped hurting, but her cheeks were hurting from laughing so hard." Chelsea frowned. "I remember all of that as clearly as if it happened yesterday. But I had to go somewhere a few days later, and I missed her passing. I thought I had longer ... and then I didn't."

"That's sad, Mommy. But you got to say goodbye that day. I know she loved it. I can feel it."

"Thanks, baby."

"Mommy, you remember things with Jocelyn. Maybe those were good memories to start with."

A smile crossed Chelsea's face. "You're right … those seem to be my strongest memories. Maybe it's because she's so important to me."

"Let's try this one." Pointing at a picture of a hot air balloon, Karsyn smiled. "Did you and Aunt Joss fly in this?"

"We did! It was the hot air balloon festival that fall. That's the last time I remember going."

"We went last year, Mommy, but you said I couldn't get in the balloon."

"We did?"

"Yes. Maybe it just wasn't that exciting."

"No, I'm sure it was … it's just … let's keep going."

Karsyn flipped forward a couple pages. "I love this picture!"

"Oh, yeah! That time I rode an elephant in India!"

"Mommy, that's Aunt Joss. You can't pretend to remember things. I know everything in here."

"I wasn't pretending. I thought I remembered riding an elephant."

"Aunt Joss. Look at her hair. She had a pixie cut. I don't know why they call it that. I don't think she looks like a pixie. She's too big."

"You're right. She doesn't look like a pixie." On the page opposite the picture of Joss, Chelsea was leaning against a sign with a big cupcake and a mermaid on it. "That must be when we first got the sign for the bakery."

"Do you remember it? I wasn't there when they put it up. I was just an egg. But you told me before that the guy picked it up with his crane and almost dropped it because a string broke."

"A cable? On the lift?" Chelsea touched the picture. She looked over every photo on the two pages. She barely remembered something about the cable breaking, but she couldn't picture like she was there when it did. There was something about that elephant, though ... elephants again ... She gasped.

"Mommy?"

"Hang on ..." Chelsea whispered. Her mind had just taken her back to the morning that Jocelyn had arrived, right before the accident. The sisters stood by the boat, surprised by how much they looked alike. Then she flashed forward to the car being slammed by the truck, grabbing her sister's hand, the elephant key chain swinging on the purse as it catapulted to the floor. "It's the elephant. That's what Zara meant."

"Who is Zara?"

"A friend," Chelsea smiled at Karsyn, tears welling up in her eyes again. It was all starting to make sense ... finally. "Karsyn, let's go see Aunt Joss ... I need to check something."

Heart pounding, Chelsea stood up and scooped Karsyn into her arms.

"Do you miss Aunt Joss because we were looking at pictures of her?"

"I do. But I remembered something, and I want to see if I'm right."

"Can you tell me? I'm good at keeping secrets."

"Let's just let it be a surprise." Chelsea winked at Karsyn, but her stomach started fluttering. *What if I'm right?* She looked down at her pajamas. "Let's change into something we can run to the hospital in."

As she scooped up her purse, she touched the tiny pink elephant keychain that hung from the zipper. *This little guy right here ... wow.* Chelsea and Karsyn jogged down the stairs and out to the car.

The drive to the hospital couldn't go fast enough. Thoughts raced through Chelsea's head as she pieced together. Her past ... the elephant ... the bakery ... Damon ... it all made so much sense if her hunch was correct.

"Everything is OK. Breathe," a voice whispered in her ear. Arms wrapped around her like she was being hugged while she drove.

"Thanks Zara ..." Chelsea whispered.

In the parking garage, Chelsea grabbed Karsyn's hand and walked quickly toward the hospital entrance. Then, she spotted a black Jeep. Slowing her walk, she stared for a moment. Her heart quickened. "Is that—?"

Resuming her pace, Chelsea put on her game face. *I have to figure out if I'm right. I have to focus.* She squeezed the little one's hand and looked at her warmly. "I'm glad you're by my side for all this."

"Me too, Mommy."

At the hospital, Mommy and daughter entered Jocelyn's room. Chelsea took in the sight of her sister slowly. Physically, they were so much alike... the same build ... the same determined but fragile jaw ... the same hair ... the same bold eyebrows ... the same gentle curve of their pink lips. It was like looking in a mirror.

No wonder people always confused us if our hairstyles weren't different ...

Karsyn ran over to Jocelyn and wrapped her arms around her. She buried her face in her neck and sighed. "I love you Aunt Joss. Wake up please."

Chelsea pulled open the drawer of the end table and took out Jocelyn's purse. No elephant key chain on this one. The same purse ... no key chain.

Her memory flashed back to a moment in the car a few minutes before the wreck ...

She dug in her purse. "You probably won't need this." She dropped something into her sister's hand.

"How cute!" It was a small rose quartz carved elephant attached to a key chain. She looked at the treasure and smiled.

"I picked it up when I was in Bali at their safari park. It reminded me of you."

"I love it! Now we won't get our purses mixed up."

The conversation echoed in her mind. "I picked it up in Bali. At the safari park." She picked up the keychain on her purse. "It reminded me of her." She gazed at the woman in the bed.

One of the machines started beeping faster.

"Karsyn ... I think you're right," Chelsea said.

"Mommy, I feel Joss's heart."

The woman in the bed twitched.

Karsyn jumped back. Chelsea pressed the call button for the nurse.

A moment later, a young woman with a blonde bun rushed in. "Did you call for me?"

"She ... she moved," Chelsea stammered. She pointed at the bed and put both hands over her mouth. "My sister ..."

"Right," the nurse responded. She fidgeted with a tablet and peeked at the heart monitor. "Her heart rate just went up a bit. It's good though."

A loud breath came from the bed, and they all turned. Jocelyn opened her eyes. She looked glazed over, confused, unfocused.

Karsyn grabbed her arm and squealed. Jocelyn looked down at her and mouthed something. Then, in a dry voice, she said, "Baby." She grabbed Karsyn's arm weakly and let out a long breath, closing her eyes again.

Inhaling loudly, Chelsea sighed as tears streamed down her face. "Sis!" She put a hand on her sister's cheek. Color was flooding back into her face. She felt warmer.

Again, Jocelyn's eyes fluttered open. The nurse held a cup up to her mouth and offered her a drink. Jocelyn raised a weak hand, but then lowered it again and allowed the nurse to dribble some water into her mouth. "I'm OK, love," she whispered. Timidly, she raised her hand again and stroked Karsyn's cheek.

Chelsea's stomach dropped. It was true. She suspected that something was up ... and it was the elephant that brought it all back to her. She had to say something. "I think there's been a mistake here."

The nurse looked surprised. "Should I get someone to talk to you about her case?"

"No, no. That's not what the mistake is. I think there was a mix-up." Chelsea put a hand on Karsyn's shoulder. "I think you were right. I'm not you're mommy. I'm Aunt Joss."

Chapter Twenty-Two

Karsyn looked nervously from the woman beside her to the woman in bed and back again.

"It's OK, Karse. I didn't know. I just thought that I was your mom because that's what everyone at the hospital told me." She succumbed to her tears as her world flipped upside-down again. "And I loved being with you the past couple weeks ... so much. I'm actually glad it happened like that, so you didn't have to worry about your mommy."

"I thought you smelled funny! No one smells like my mommy," Karsyn leaned back down and buried her face in the real Chelsea's hair.

Chelsea smiled weakly and patted Karsyn's back. "So what did I miss? You'll have to explain."

"You are my mommy. You smell right," Karsyn said.

Jocelyn sat down, overwhelmed by her discovery. "You've heard of babies being switched at birth, right?"

Chelsea chuckled. "Yeah."

"Well, we were switched at our thirty-fifth birthday."

"Seems like we're a little old for people to get us confused."

"That's what I thought. I just spent the last two weeks thinking I was you and wondering why I couldn't remember anything right." Jocelyn's overwhelm was getting the best of her. She sobbed loudly. "I'm so glad it happened though. I was there with Karsyn the whole time."

"I've been here for two weeks?" Chelsea asked.

Jocelyn briefed her on the details of the accident.

"Whoa. Are you OK?" she asked.

"I just got a glimpse of a life that I was never meant to live. And ... I don't know. I wonder what I missed in my real life. I wonder how I'm going to get back into that. I just ... there's so much."

"I know," Chelsea said. "When can I go home?" she asked the nurse.

"Maybe a couple days," the nurse said. She was rapidly typing on the tablet. "I'm bringing the doctor in to check you over. I'm glad you're up." Warmly, the nurse touched her arm and then left, presumably to get the doctor.

"You know," Karsyn said, "I knew something was wrong. You used Mommy's shampoo, but you still didn't smell like Mommy."

"That's true," Jocelyn said. "I've been using all the same stuff that your mom uses but it must smell different on her. Maybe identical twins are more different than everyone thinks."

"Places leave their mark on you," Chelsea said.

"That's true," Jocelyn said. "I might smell like the world, but you smell like home." She sobbed again loudly and wrapped her arms around her sister and her niece. "I'm so glad you're OK!"

For the next hour, Jocelyn and Karsyn filled Chelsea in on their time while she was sleeping. The doctor came in and said she needed forty-eight hours for monitoring, but she should be good to go home Wednesday evening and rest if everything checked out. Her bruised rib and random cuts were already mostly healed, and she seemed healthy. Her arm still needed a few more weeks in the cast. She didn't want to take any chances and release Chelsea early though.

After the doctor left, Jocelyn—the real Jocelyn—took on a sober look. There was way more that had happened since the wreck ... and much was left up in the air. She hoped she hadn't messed up Chelsea's life too badly. At least the bakery was still standing.

"Hey ... there's something I need to fix." Jocelyn picked up Chelsea's purse. The elephant swung back and forth wisely as she dug out the phone. Then she scooped up her own purse. "Mind if I borrow my phone?"

Chelsea shook her head. "What are you doing?"

Plugging the phone into the wall, Jocelyn grinned. "Trust me. It's pretty important." After a moment, the phone had enough power to work. She typed the password. "See, I remember *my* password. I had to find that book of passwords you keep in your desk to do your phone's password. I'm glad you told me where it was ..."

"Always good to be prepared. You never know when you'll think you're me and have memory loss, right?"

Jocelyn grinned. She picked up Chelsea's phone, searched for a moment and then punched something into her own phone. "Be right back." She dashed out of the room, placing her phone against her ear.

In the hallway, Jocelyn listened to the phone ringing, praying that there would be an answer.

"OmniDigital Design, this is Julian Vega."

He must think it's a business call. "Hey, this is Jocelyn. Chelsea's sister."

"You're awake?" He sounded surprised but then switched to a dry tone. "I'm glad to hear that you're better."

"Listen ... I know you probably don't want to hear from me, but I have the absolute strangest thing to tell you. Let me explain ..." She briefed him on the events of the evening and was greeted with silence. "Are you still there?"

"That's a lot to take in."

"Trust me. I lived it, and *I* think it's a lot to take in."

Silence.

Finally, Julian said softly, "Can I see her?"

Jocelyn grinned. "Of course. She doesn't know that I called you. Just come. Now."

When she re-entered the hospital room, she found Karsyn sitting on Chelsea's bed telling her excitedly about everything she had missed. Chelsea looked tired, but she smiled and held Karsyn's hand.

Jocelyn felt her heart ache. Just hours before, she thought that Karsyn was hers. That was her world. For a few brief days, she had the wonder of being a mother. Now that Karsyn was back in her sister's hands, she was starting to feel a strange emptiness inside her chest.

Hand over her heart, she watched the mother and daughter for a moment, feeling the love between the two of them. Not feeling a part of that now was ... strange. And she didn't know if that's something she would ever feel again.

Chelsea looked over at her and smiled. "You OK?"

Jocelyn sat heavily in the chair. "I am. I'm just so glad that you're back with us." She could save discussion of any deeper feelings for later when Chelsea was home where she belonged and had time to relax. That odd tug in her heart would wait.

A short time later, the door opened. Chelsea turned and gasped. "Julian."

"So no one was crazy. Just wanted to mention that," Jocelyn laughed.

Julian chuckled. "I'm just glad she remembers me." He appeared to be overwhelmed with love as he took Chelsea's hand and stared deeply into her eyes, his own eyes welling up with tears.

Chelsea looked suspiciously at Jocelyn. "You've met?"

"We actually thought that we were dating. It was super awkward," Jocelyn explained. "Luckily, we didn't kiss. You're all good. He's yours." She winked at Chelsea, and Julian laughed.

"Can't wait to hear that story!" Chelsea said. Then she turned to Karsyn. "Cupcake, I'd like you to meet Julian. This isn't how I planned on you two meeting, but here we are. We've been dating for a few months, and I thought it was time for me to introduce you anyway. He's my boyfriend."

Karsyn looked at him like she was judging him. "What's your job? Do you have your own car?"

"Good questions," Julian said. He started to answer, so Jocelyn slipped from the room, letting her sister have some family time.

Pulling out her phone, Jocelyn noted the time. Her stomach rumbled. She texted Julian.

"I'm picking up dinner. Be back soon. You guys hang out."

Then, she sat down on a bench outside of the hospital and watched the setting sun, feeling exceedingly tired.

"So that's it. Now I have to figure out my life again." A life that had been left behind for two weeks while she struggled to catch up with her sister's life. She closed her eyes and leaned her head back. Now the two lives mingled together in her mind, in their warmth, excitement, and love. How would she get back to where she had been? When?

Did she want to?

Sighing, she opened her eyes again. "I guess I can live in the moment for one more night." Standing, she pulled her phone back out and called Saperi's for pizza.

Back in the parking garage, Jocelyn hopped in her car and drove to the nearest convenience store for bottled water and paper plates, hoping to beat the pizza guy back to the hospital. As she walked back to the car with her bag, she slowed down. The evening air was full of possibility as it blew the salty sea air across the island playing with the ends of her hair. Jocelyn breathed deeply. What a crazy day.

She got back in her car. *Focus. It's pizza and family time.* She smiled. A warm, fuzzy feeling came over her as she realized that she had her sister back and no idea what the future held. But she didn't need to run any more. This was home. She would figure out the rest.

Chapter Twenty-Three

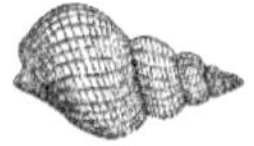

Back in the hospital parking garage, Jocelyn parked the car and realized that this wasn't *her* rental. She was suddenly firmly in her true body, but now everything was "borrowed." Laughing, she looked down at her cotton shorts, t-shirt, and cardigan. "Yep, borrowed. Glad Chelse and I are at least the same size." *That would have been so strange if I thought I was Chelsea and then couldn't fit in any of her clothes.*

Gathering her bags, she hopped out of the car and then gasped. "The boots ..." *Zara must have been saying that the clothes weren't the right fit. That I'm not me.* "I think I actually have those boots in my flat," she murmured. The memory of her tiny apartment in Mannheim, Germany flooded back to her. The local artwork on the walls. Her meager belongings. Over a decade of frequent travel meant that everything was borrowed.

Maybe it was time for something of her own.

Walking to the front door of the hospital, Jocelyn made a point of really feeling the breeze flipping her hair. Seeing everything from the sun dipping low in the sky to the lavender bushes covered in flowers, dancing in the wind. Their scent mingled with the salt air, the sweetest, most welcoming scent there is. Jocelyn stopped and just breathed.

This. This right here. This is where I belong. Maybe the world needs to wait a little longer.

Entering the hospital, Jocelyn looked at her phone. Pizza should be here any minute. She stepped off to the side and admired an abstract painting in blues, white, and gold that reminded her of the sea, of all the shores she had braved.

For some reason, this one had been the toughest.

In her own world, she didn't realize that someone was walking quickly down the hall behind her, and she smacked right into him as she paced.

"Oh. Geez. I'm so sorry. I wasn't paying attention—" she started.

"No, you're good—Hey!"

"Adrian. Hi. What are you doing here?"

"All the cool kids hang out at the hospital." Adrian chuckled. "I'm dropping off my nephews. My sister-in-law is a pediatrician up on the fifth floor. I took the boys to a baseball game tonight, and my brother is caught at his job still. Kaci asked me to just drop them here, since she's almost done."

"That's so nice. I bet they really enjoyed that."

"They did. Especially the pretzels, hot dogs, soda, ice cream, nachos ..."

"Ha. I guess you spoil them."

"It's a Fierro tradition. My siblings did it for me when I was little, so I'm returning the favor." Suddenly Adrian got serious. "So how's your sister?"

Jocelyn grinned. "Funny story ... remember my memory problem? It was actually because I thought I was someone else."

Adrian stared at her blankly. "So you don't have a sister?"

"I do. But I thought I was her. I was driving her car when we wrecked, so the hospital thought I was Chelsea. We look enough alike that everyone just believed them."

"That's crazy. How did you find out?"

"I—oh! Pizza is here. Excuse me a second." Jocelyn tipped the pizza guy and took the pie.

"Here. Can I help you with that?" Adrian held out his hands for the pizza.

"Actually, yes, I'd love the help. Are you busy right now?"

"I don't have plans, but I definitely don't need anything to eat." They both laughed and started walking toward the elevators.

"Chelsea is upstairs with Karsyn—her daughter, not mine. Also, um, Julian is there."

"Do I know Julian?"

"He's Chelsea's boyfriend, who I didn't know about till after the wreck. I asked him for some distance because I thought we were an item but didn't feel it and didn't want to ruin anything that I had before in case my feelings came back ... which it turns out I never had in the first place because he's actually my sister's boyfriend. Really glad I didn't have any feelings for him, by the way. That would be really strange now."

"OK, let me catch up. So, you thought you had a boyfriend, but you didn't like him?" He frowned.

"Didn't have feelings for him. He's really nice. Just ... no chemistry. Thank goodness." She paused and glanced sideways at Adrian. "So, I asked for space. And he's the one who came in the bakery when we were talking."

Adrian laughed. "Oh. Well, that explains that. This is getting stranger by the minute."

"Thanks for sticking around for it. I'm sure it is bizarre."

"It explains a lot of your behavior though. I imagine you were confused about it in the middle of trying to just be a good mom and run your bakery."

"You're right. And I felt like there was something between *us*, so I was doubly confused and didn't want anyone to get hurt." Jocelyn let out a huge breath. "I didn't want to say 'no' when you asked me out, but I also didn't want to hurt you or Julian."

"That's a lot to deal with." Adrian looked sympathetically at Jocelyn. "So how is your sister doing?"

The elevator door opened, and they both entered. "Chelsea is OK now. She woke up this evening. And she remembers who she is. Which is great. And it confirmed what I realized today—that we had unintentionally traded places."

The two got in the elevator, and Jocelyn pressed the button for the third floor.

"Wow." Adrian leaned against the wall and shook his head in amazement. "And how does Julian feel about all this?"

Jocelyn laughed. "He was actually thrilled to find out he wasn't dating me. Imagine that."

Adrian smiled at her. "Yeah, imagine that. So who are you exactly? I don't believe we've actually met."

"Jocelyn Bloom. I live in Mannheim, Germany, right now, and I was about to start a six-week stint filming my show *Braving Borders* all over Germany. I have some people to check in with tomorrow to figure out what was going on with that and how to get back on schedule with filming."

"That all makes sense now. And I was telling the truth when I said I've watched your show. You're brilliant. I love the little places you find to take your viewers. So unusual. I recently watched the Bali episode with the elephants."

"That's one of my favorites."

As they got off the elevator, Jocelyn got quiet as she felt her heart grow heavy. Her real life would be starting up again soon. Too soon. And here was all this possibility in front of her. She always thought she had to be halfway around the world for an adventure, to be brave, but maybe it was only an arm-length away ...

Adrian must have felt it too because he stopped and looked at her. "I don't expect you to have an answer right now, and I know that we just met. But the person I've known over the past couple weeks is someone I truly would like to know better ... and you might be going back to Europe soon. Just letting you know what's on my mind. I understand if you want to jump back into your life. It sounds pretty exciting. I just think you're special, and I feel like this could be the start of something amazing ... if you'll be around and want to try."

Jocelyn's breath caught, and she gazed into his eyes, wondering if crossing the ocean would be worth not being able to lose herself in them again and often. "I feel like we haven't even started, and then I find out that it's not a possibility because of what my life was before." She looked determined. "But, really, I make my own magic. I always have. What I have realized over the past couple weeks is that I put everything on hold so I could chase my dreams around the world, thinking I could only have one or the other. Being with my sister and my niece and *believing* in my heart that she was my daughter really put things in perspective. I'll be thirty-five tomorrow, and I have only lived part of the life I wanted, pushing away relationships because adventure was at the top of the list. I think I finally realize what I've been missing."

Adrian's eyes softened. "That's a lot to process, but I get it. I've been pretty busy with my career and playing uncle, which is fun. Don't get me wrong. But when we danced the other night, I felt something inside me that I haven't felt in a long time. I'd like to see where this goes, if possible."

Jocelyn wrapped her arm around Adrian in a sideways hug. "I think I need to change my home base to Sorel Island. This is my home, and this is where I want to be when I'm not filming. I'd certainly love to see where things go with us. It's definitely time for me to make some new memories here."

Balancing the pizza on one hand, Adrian wrapped an arm around Jocelyn's waist. "I'd like that too."

Jocelyn gazed adoringly at Adrian for a moment, silently hoping that he would kiss her. She smiled coyly and glanced away. When she looked back, she knew he was thinking the same thing. She tipped her head and glanced at his lips.

Grinning, Adrian read the obvious signal, pulled her closer with one arm, and kissed her.

The smell of his cologne enveloped her as her heart fluttered uncontrollably in her chest. Reaching up, she ran her hand along his jaw and thought she would melt right there.

When Adrian finally pulled back from her lips, the pair continued to gaze at each other.

"Don't drop the pizza," Jocelyn whispered. Then she winked and continued down the hall to her family with Adrian right behind her.

Chapter Twenty-Four

"Time to slow down," Jocelyn said to herself.

The wind rippled her hair like a field of wheat as the boat decelerated to dock on Sorel Island.

Déjà vu overtook her as she gathered her bags and left the boat, searching for Chelsea among those mingling by the parking lot. A flash of sun reflected on a car pulling into the lot, which caught her attention. "That must be her." A little late, but whatever. They had all the time in the world for the next few weeks.

Jocelyn walked over to a piling and waited till she was certain that the silver-gray car was really Chelsea's. A moment later, she saw a willowy blonde woman emerge from the car and help a child from the back. *Yep, that's them!*

Cheerfully, Chelsea waved, and Karsyn skipped along wildly, holding her mother's hand. Jocelyn waved back and started across the lot lugging her things.

"It's a lot hotter than a couple months ago!" Jocelyn said. She embraced her sister and her niece at the same time.

Chelsea took the stacked rolling suitcases from her sister, and they all continued toward the car. "It's July. It's always hot here after the fourth."

"It's almost my birthday!" Karsyn exclaimed.

"I know, cupcake!" Jocelyn grabbed Karsyn's hand and spun her around. "That's why I'm here. I had to be back to celebrate with you."

"I'm having a pink poodle cake and lots of presents. You've got to see the cake. It's so super cool!"

"Pink poodle?" Jocelyn said.

"She wanted a 'fancy' cake, so I searched Pinterest. That's what she liked," Chelsea laughed.

"I see," Jocelyn stopped by the car. "Another one, huh?"

"Of course, I got the same thing. I loved the last one," Chelsea said.

"Of course," Jocelyn said, hopping in the passenger seat. "But I'll let you drive this time."

Chelsea got in and squeezed Jocelyn's hand. The pair met each other's gaze with a stiff smile. "I still can't believe we went through that."

"I think we're stronger for it," Jocelyn said. "I'm definitely changed. I think it happened *for* us."

"I'm glad for the change," Chelsea said. She backed the car out of the spot and drove them all back to the townhouse.

Later, after Karsyn was in bed, Chelsea and Jocelyn each got a glass of wine and went out on the balcony of Chelsea's room.

After a sip of the white zin, Jocelyn leaned on the railing and spoke as if she were talking to the night.

"Maybe that was the Universe's way of protecting Karsyn through this whole mess. Just think how different it would have been if she knew you were the one in the hospital."

"Yeah. I'm glad you were here for her … pretending to be me," Chelsea chuckled. "At least the kid wasn't scared. That would have turned her life upside down." She paused. "Especially after I split with Damon, that would have been hard."

"Speaking of me 'pretending to be you,'" Jocelyn sat in one of the chairs. "Do you think maybe Karsyn knew deep down all the time."

"I don't know." Chelsea joined her in the other chair. "She's clever, but if she knew, I don't think she would have kept quiet about it. She would have been scared for me. And she isn't good at keeping secrets."

"True."

They sat in silence for a few minutes.

"I'm glad you're here," Chelsea said.

"I'm looking forward to a new adventure," Jocelyn answered. She swirled her wine in her glass. "Glad I found a way to make it all work!"

"Me too," Chelsea said. "Really. I've been hoping for this for years."

After breakfast the next morning, Chelsea, Jocelyn, and Karsyn loaded party supplies in the car and drove to The Salty Cupcake. Karsyn practically ran inside, dragging Jocelyn behind her.

"You have to see my cake!"

"Yes! Can't wait!" Jocelyn play-jogged, pumping her arms goofily as she followed Karsyn to the kitchen door.

The women both waved at Isabel, who was at the register, and Chelsea pushed open the kitchen door.

"At least I know all the staff and how everything works here now," Jocelyn said.

"That's going to help. Sorry you had to go through the training the way you did," Chelsea said.

"Good morning ladies!" Samantha greeted them in the kitchen. "And happy birthday, kiddo!" She booped Karsyn's nose.

"Thank you! Can I see the cake?" Karsyn jumped up and down.

Samantha winked and turned back to the counter. Gently, she lifted the cake and then squatted so Karsyn could get the full view. Chelsea firmly grabbed Karsyn's shoulder to keep her distance.

"I love it! Aunt Joss, isn't it cool?"

The cake had a pink poodle traipsing past the Eiffel Tower with a bunch of balloons iced on it. "Happy sixth birthday Karsyn!" was written in pink icing across the cake.

"Holy moly," Jocelyn said. "Are you going to expect me to do that?"

Chelsea laughed. "Not yet. You can try when you're ready … if you want to. For now, let's just stick with what you know. I'm so glad to have an extra set of hands in the kitchen."

"This lined up great with Tara moving, too. We needed another part-time manager," Samantha said. "Between the boys and the bagels, I'm fried."

"Ha!" Jocelyn said. "I see what you did there."

"Actually, you don't fry bagels." Chelsea patted Jocelyn on the shoulder.

"I have things to learn," Jocelyn laughed.

Suddenly Chelsea pulled out her phone. "Damon says he will meet us at the park at ten thirty to set up." She looked up at Jocelyn. "Party starts at eleven. Pizza should be there at noon."

"Perfect. Then we sugar the kids up and send them home," Jocelyn said.

"We will do our best to stay the whole time," Samantha said. "Elliot usually naps around one, so he may get cranky."

"I totally understand," Chelsea said.

Jocelyn looked at her phone, read the text message that had popped up, and smiled joyfully. "We should get going. It's ten twenty."

Chelsea sighed happily. "I love seeing you smile like that. The last time I saw you that happy was when Karsyn was born."

"It's nice to dream ... and be adored," Jocelyn responded. She dropped her phone back into her purse and picked up the cake.

"I'll see you guys in a bit!" Samantha called as the trio exited the bakery.

A few minutes later, they pulled into the lot by the Willow Pavilion at Bottle Beach.

"I've never been so terrified in my life." Jocelyn lifted the cake from her lap and hoisted herself out of the car. "I hope I don't have to hold the leftover cake on the way home."

"I plan on eating the leftover cake while the kids wait for their parents," Chelsea said.

"I'm going to eat a HUGE piece! There won't be any leftovers!" Karsyn announced. She ran to greet her father and leapt into his arms.

"Happy birthday, sweetie!" Damon said. He crushed the little one in an over-the-top hug and then swung her around.

Karsyn squealed with delight.

"Ready to help decorate?" he said.

"No, I'm just here to swing," Karsyn ran over to the swing set near the pavilion and did her thing.

"She's honest," Jocelyn said. For a moment, she watched her niece swinging without a care, her hair billowing around her as she swung back and forth. Then she scooped up a roll of streamers and started making birthday magic.

In just a few minutes, the pavilion was ready for a six-year-old's birthday party with cake, table covers, streamers, and balloons.

"That looks great! Nice job you guys!" Karsyn called from the swings.

Chelsea curtseyed while the other two just laughed.

Just then, a blue sedan car pulled up.

"Julian," Chelsea called. He pulled a huge gift bag from the back seat of the car and approached the pavilion. She put an arm around him and gave him a quick peck.

"Hey Jocelyn, Damon," Julian said. He set the gift bag on a table.

Damon stepped forward and shook Julian's hand. "I suppose I should congratulate you."

"Thank you," Julian said. "I appreciate that."

Chelsea smiled at Jocelyn, "You'll be back in town again for the wedding, right? You promised."

"I already arranged my shooting schedule so I will be in Slovakia at the beginning of September and then back here a few days before the big day," Jocelyn answered. "I promise. Again."

Chelsea threw her arms around Jocelyn. "I'm just so glad to have you here with us permanently! This is really the best birthday gift ever."

"Thanks! And if you want to give me a late birthday gift, you can help me find a place to live this week." Jocelyn laughed. "If I'm going to live here, I can't crash at your place forever."

Guests started to arrive, parents with wild kindergarteners running ahead of them to the playground. Karsyn played hostess by lovingly squeezing every child who showed up and then taking their hand and running to the play yard.

As Karsyn's parents and Julian chatted with the other parents, Jocelyn ventured away from the party toward the beach. With the din of happy children playing behind her, she focused on the crashing waves and sat in the sand.

Traveling around the world, exploring new places felt like the biggest accomplishment to her for a long time. Being here now, after being a "mom" and really enjoying calling a place home, she realized that there were things she didn't even realize she missed.

When nothing is permanent, you go into each new city brave. Knowing that you may never see those people again, you don't get attached. You always feel like you belong but don't, like the wind may blow you away to a new place any moment, and you'll have to get your bearings again.

You stop laying down roots. You stop going deep. With the earth. With the people. With yourself.

Over the years, this lifestyle gives you a lot of time to reflect on the intricacies and the beauty in every part of the world, but it leaves little time or desire for introspection.

That's what she wanted for so long.

But now, what she wanted more than anything was to keep discovering who she was ... and to let someone else delve deep into knowing her as well.

Plumbing the depths of your soul is something best left for times when you can fully appreciate and love yourself. Times when you can feel the earth below, smell the sea, and witness the clouds above in their never-ending dance across the heavens.

Times like now.

Jocelyn suddenly found herself on the verge of tears with the beauty of everything in her life. In just a few months, she had re-awakened a desire to belong and had actively sought a home-base that let her do just that.

And also continue the career she loved.

Because wanderlust doesn't just fizzle with the feeling of being rooted.

She smiled crookedly. This must be what they call "balance."

The salty air hung heavy around her on this hot day, but in the shade of the tree where she sat, she didn't mind.

A breeze flirted with the hem of her sundress.

"Joss?"

Turning, she waved brightly. "Yeah, I'm here!"

In a bright red Henley that showed off his olive skin, Adrian stood out against the trees and the sand. It fit the curves of his muscular chest and arms just right. Jocelyn couldn't help but admire him as he approached.

"Join me," she patted the sand beside her.

As he sat, he wrapped an arm around her shoulders. Then he leaned in and kissed her lips gently. "It's good to see you again."

Jocelyn felt a shiver go through her body, let out a long sigh, and leaned against him. "You too," she said dreamily. The thrill of being with someone, finally, after so long on her own, raced through her. She looked up at Adrian and let herself just get lost in dreams of what the future might hold. Between the sun and the sea, she was ready to take the first few steps down the path of the unknown ... a romance that would let her explore love.

"Pizza!" Chelsea suddenly yelled from the pavilion.

"Come on. We should go help," Jocelyn said.

Adrian found her hand, and the two walked back to the pavilion.

A thump on her thigh made Jocelyn stop and place her hand on her dress pocket. Something lumpy was in there.

Adrian watched her curiously.

Jocelyn frowned and reached into the pocket. When she pulled her hand out, she was holding a perfectly smooth piece of sea glass the size of a half dollar.

A shiver chased down her spine, and she knew, at that moment, that everything had gone according to plan ... and that everything would just work out for her.

"Sea glass." She held it so Adrian could see. "Not sure how it got there."

Adrian shrugged and brushed a stray hair from Jocelyn's face. "This is Bottle Beach, after all. Magical things happen here."

Jocelyn slipped her hand back into Adrian's— feeling her heart flutter with glee—and proceeded back to the party. "Thanks, Zara," she whispered.

Discussion Guide

1. Is there anything different you would have done to discover your past if you were Chelsea?
2. Should Chelsea have kept her confusion about Julian and her feelings for him hidden? How would the story have played out differently if she had?
3. Did you suspect that Chelsea and Jocelyn had switched lives? Why or why not?
4. Why do you think Chelsea never mentioned Zara to Samantha?
5. Why do you think the author chose *Braving the Shore* as the title of the book, and what does it mean to you?
6. Do you have a special place you go to think, clear your head, or find peace, like Chelsea at the beach?
7. Do you have meaningful childhood memories of family vacations spots, like Bottle Beach? What do they mean to you now?
8. Do you have an object or symbol that holds special meaning for you, like the sea glass in the story? What is it and why is it important?
9. What does it mean to be brave?
10. Do you have a Zara in your life?
11. Have you ever applied themes from your dreams to real life? Have you made any important connections?
12. What lessons can you take away from this story and apply to your lives?

The complete opposite of a comfort zone …
Kenzi reluctantly participates in an
archaeological dig in her hunt for

The Treasures We Seek

Keep reading for an excerpt from the next book in the
Soul Sisterhood Series.

Chapter One

"That's the third one this month ..." I gaze into the mirror at yet another gray hair. I'm getting ready for work and spot it shimmering rebelliously in the sea of my dark brown tresses, sprouting right from the part, looking like a piece of tinsel on a bitter dark chocolate bar.

Festive.

Scientifically speaking, I know I can't blame the gray hair on stress. I know it's genetic. And I also know that I'm blessed in that department. Neither of my parents had much gray till their fifties, so I know I have time.

But that doesn't make me feel any less urgent to get my act together. I started to a few months ago, but you know ...

Nothing like a good shake up in "the plans"—life plans, all the stuff that you're supposed to do, including a house, family, six-figure job, burnout, etc.—to make you feel a little on edge. God, I just turned thirty. Sometimes I feel like my clock is tick tick ticking ... and I still haven't gotten my life figured out.

I know what you're thinking. It's not like I live in my mom's basement. I let out a huge sigh as the internal battle wages on. I own a duplex. And I have a job that I love.

And no, *a job* doesn't make you a grownup. And it doesn't mean that you're fulfilled and satisfied. It literally means that you're employed.

Again, I know I'm lucky in that department. I smile, recalling how much I love what I do. I breathe it. I sweat it. I live it.

And that's kind of the problem ...

I wouldn't say that I'm a workaholic, *per se*, but given the options, an hour of overtime is waaaay more appealing than happy hour.

And so is a good book. Or movie. I'm not terribly picky about how I spend my alone time.

But we're *supposed* to do what makes us happy, right? And if happiness to me is sketching a new home or spending an entire Saturday with my nose in a book or grabbing a glass of wine and chatting with Macy and Lauren, then why worry?

I keep asking myself that. *Why worry? Am I worried?* Maybe. *A tad? A skosh?* I know by this point I was supposed to have fallen head over heels for someone, my hand weighed down with an obligatory giant diamond, and have two to five kids and a minivan <shudder>, but is that for me?

What about my purpose? What *is* a purpose? And why can't someone just email me with it?

I decided after my disastrous last relationship ... which ended about a year ago, a story for another time ... that the head over heels thing sounds incredibly painful, debilitating, life-threatening even. Who wants a concussion? And wasn't there an author who said that she would never fall in love because the men in her books, the ones she creates, are way better than real men anyway? That no living man could ever stand up to the man on the page? Something like that.

So, what's the point?

I haven't sworn off men. I look. I admire. I just don't feel that uterus-pulsing desire to grab a "good one" and pop out babies. (My brother has four, which is technically enough for both of us.) I did feel that once. But honestly, I prefer my job: chatting with a couple about their perfect home and then making it happen for them is so much more satisfying than chatting with a stranger about his perfect future and deciding that I'm too much my own woman to just cave and draw it for him. Being an architect is about making dreams come true. It's about being a people pleaser, and I'm cool with that. That's easy.

Being a girlfriend is not.

Sorry, not sorry.

Relationships don't work when one person is a people pleaser and the other is, well, taking advantage. I've done that before.

God, I need a lot of concealer today. Serious dark circles. What the hell? I didn't even think the weekend was that rough.

I did Thanksgiving with Lauren's family across town this year, and Macy came with, since her parents are visiting family in Kenya right now and her siblings are scattered all over the US.

Lauren's family was so welcoming to us Thanksgiving orphans. And Mom and Stan will be back in Pittsburgh for Christmas, so it wasn't a huge deal that I didn't see them.

But here's the snag. Mom wants to do Christmas *at my house*. My tiny half of the duplex. Maybe it's not so tiny. But it's still a lot of people to host. Mom, Stan, Grandma Claudia, Declan and Sarah, and their four kids ... And me, of course. She called last night to ask me. I mean *tell* me. But she made it sound like she was asking.

I'm sure I can do it. I'm just nervous because I've never done it before. Since my brother Declan got married, it's just been easier to do it at his house ... with all the kids. Sarah said it's really hard to get all their stuff together and drag them around. But they are all out of diapers now, so that's less stuff. In fact, the kids became so portable this year that Declan and Sarah took them all to Paris for the fall to live in a cute little apartment and learn French and eat pastries, and wow, the pictures are gorgeous.

He's a business coach, so he has that kind of flexibility. And Sarah manages a social media management company. Makes it all easy. They just put team members in place to help out with the biz and hired a sweet older French lady, Marguerite, to home school the littles and handle some of the cooking and cleaning, *s'il vous plait*.

Anyway, Declan is living the dream, but their Pittsburgh house is rented out till the twenty-second, so they aren't leaving Europe till the twenty-third. Who knows if they will get over the jetlag, let alone put up Christmas decorations in time! Mom wants things to be perfect. I get it. I can host Christmas. No sweat, right?

It's just an extra *nine* people to cook for ... and over half of them are used to having French cuisine prepared for them every day. *Welcome! Grilled cheese, anyone?* Bon appétit!

Where's my lipstick? In my purse. Right. I threw it in last night.

Now where did I set my purse? Probably in my bedroom.

My bed is neatly made up with my new winter comforter. It's white. Like snow. And I've tossed a gray furry throw jauntily across the bottom corner of the bed. I love the way it drapes. A single red pillow with the word "Joy" embroidered across it graces the pair of sleeping pillows at the head of the bed. Simple and perfect.

The purse, however, is not on my bed. It's on the dresser. In fact, it's the only thing on the dresser besides the book I was reading last night, *A Holiday in the City*, which is such a great romance. Love!

I snag the lipstick from my purse and apply it quickly. Then, I grab my purse and work bag and dash to the garage.

I slip on black loafers that are waiting for me by the garage door. They look great with my outfit, which is simple and professional: black sweater, black and white houndstooth pants ... I swear I own things in other colors ... red gemstone statement necklace.

I throw on my coat, which, yes, is black, and hop in my car. Fine, the car is gray. Man, I like neutrals. It's easy to splash things up with a bright colored bag or pillow or vase or whatever and have a clean look.

The first day back at the office after Thanksgiving break is bound to be busy, but it's always a good busy. The kind of busy where you take a deep breath of your coffee, sip it slowly, and dive into your inbox in the quiet of your office.

Maybe it's weird, but I love it.

I put the car in reverse, leave the garage, and head for that quiet.

Baker & Willow is honestly a great place to work. It's the first architectural firm that took an interest in my design work and gave me a serious position designing homes instead of asking if I wanted to assist the head designers, like the bigger firms. Plus, I love that it's just outside of Pittsburgh. It's easy to get to, and I didn't have to move somewhere where I didn't know anyone to get started on my career ... seven years ago.

I've been pretty comfortable here.

Even easier: it's only a fifteen-minute drive from my development. Baker & Willow was contracted for design work in Chestnut Acres, so I had first bid on the duplex. Easy peasy.

Maybe too easy ...

But hey, it's all good right now, till I'm ready to shake things up and spread my wings.

I guide my car onto the highway and head south to the next exit. Traffic isn't terrible heading south, away from the city. The other way, no thank you! It's thick and about to get even worse. Rush hour is no joke around here.

I turn into the business park where Baker & Willow's offices are and park in the first row, close to the building. I love being an early bird ...for several reasons.

Not only do I get ah-mazing parking, but I also get to avoid a lot of the small talk with people wandering into the building to start their day.

Thanks, but no thanks. I'm happy with the quiet and not discussing the weather with that odd older guy in accounting who talks to EVERYONE about nothing.

"Good morning, Rachel!" I chirp to our receptionist. She is the sweetest lady.

Rachel smiles. "Coffee is brewing, Kenzi." She points at my empty hand. "Make sure you grab it before the rest of them get here."

"No worries with that. You're the best."

I unlock my office and slip inside. Ah, normalcy. Quiet. I drop off my stuff, slip back to the coffee station with my "PERFCT" mug—one of my birthday presents from Lauren, she's funny—and return to my desk with caffeine. Time to dive into the email.

As I peruse my inbox, a few souls straggle into the building. Half an hour later, most of my coworkers show up. It's a small company, so there aren't a ton of people anyway, but we share a parking lot with all the other businesses in the building, sooooo ... best to be early.

I don't really look up, but I notice the stream of people passing my door. A couple people tap on the glass and wave, so I wave back. It's a nice group here, and I talk with a few of them, but I'm not really close with anyone.

Around nine, I'm catching up on my to-do list, having finished my emails from break, when I hear a tap on my door. I glance up and see Logan Oliver, the head of sales and marketing, smiling and waving. He has an adorable, crooked smile with a dimple and always dresses so nice. If I weren't dead inside, that smile might make my heart flutter. Today, he's in a gray suit and tie. When I smile back, I realize he's still standing there. *Does he want to talk to me?* My smile slips. We've never said more than a few words to each other. Quickly, I grin again and motion for him to come in.

"Hey, how was Thanksgiving?" Logan says.

"Um, good. Yours?" The silence in my head will surely smother me.

He sets a plate down on my desk and sits in the spare chair without me motioning toward it. *Is he here to hang out?* Now I'm a little on edge.

"It was good. Got to see a lot of my family, so that was nice. I grew up here, so I have relatives all over the city. Did you visit family?"

"No. I went to a friend's Thanksgiving at her parents' house. My parents aren't here anymore, and my brother is out of town. It was nice, though." I play with the blue-green beaded bracelet I'm wearing, spinning it around my wrist.

"Aw, I'm sorry to hear that about your parents."

"Excuse me?"

"You said they aren't here—"

"Oh." Gah! "No, my mom and stepdad moved to Florida, and my dad is in Seattle. They are all alive and well, just not living in the area anymore."

"That's great that your friend invited you to join her family. Do you do that often?"

"I've met them a few times." Despite my best efforts to maintain my anti-social energy barrier, I feel it starting to come down. Logan is nice to talk to. "One of our other friends joined us too, since her parents are out of the country."

"That's really nice. The people of Pittsburgh are so friendly. My family welcomed in a couple of my roommates for holidays back when I was in college, and I know lots of other people who have done the same thing. That's one of the reasons I don't think I could leave this place."

"It's definitely special." I glance back at my computer, sure I should get back to my work.

Logan must have noticed because he sits forward in the chair and gestures at the plate on my desk. "Well, I know you're busy, but I stopped by because I wanted to make sure you got some banana bread. I baked it over the weekend, and I know you tend to stay in your office most of the day when you're not on site. Didn't want you to miss out."

"Oh. I appreciate it, but I'm good. I ate before I came in."

"Do you want a piece for later?"

Of course he would offer that. "Thank you, but not really."

"Ah." Logan seems disappointed, hopefully not offended. "It was nice talking to you anyway. I'll see you later." He scoops up the plate and smiles at me. It is a hard-to-read smile. Seems friendly, maybe offended. I'm sure that I'm constantly secretly offending people, especially when I turn down food.

"I'll see ya. Thanks again for stopping by." I smile and grasp for something to say to smooth things over. "Hey, by the way ... I like your tie." I actually do. It's deep blue and covered in a pattern of gingerbread boys and girls.

He glances down and grabs the tie, as if he forgot what he was wearing. "Thanks! I like to get festive early."

"Same here. See you later." I turn back to my computer as he leaves. Breathing out slowly, I frown. I sip my coffee. Man, I hate doing that. Just hope the guy isn't offended.

I notice that he hovers for a moment outside the door and then heads in the direction of the break room, probably to drop off the bread for everyone else. I feel bad, but I need to work. That was nice though! I should probably talk to my coworkers a little more often and about more than just work-related things. Maybe this is the dawn of a new Kenzi.

I'll think about it.

About the Author

Cori Wamsley is the award-winning author of the Soul Sisterhood series, best friend stories with a side of sweet romance. Her books are enchanting and witty women's fiction, woven with the magic of self-discovery, history, adventure, and falling in love.

Aside from writing books, she also runs a small publishing house, Aurora Corialis Publishing, where she helps authors write and publish their personal stories, as well as some fiction.

Cori lives in Pittsburgh, Pa., US, with her husband and two creative tween daughters. When she's not at her desk, she loves painting, crafting, playing piano, and singing. She's also into reading sweet romance and dreaming about traveling to Europe.

Follow Cori on Instagram, Threads, or TikTok @coriwamsley_author.

Learn more at www.coriwamsley.com.

Soul Sisterhood Series

For more best friend stories with a side of sweet romance, check out the other books in the Soul Sisterhood series!

www.ingramcontent.com/pod-product-compliance
Lightning Source LLC
Chambersburg PA
CBHW021646110726
47902CB00007B/1853